DEAD TO SIN

Nicholas Penn is summoned to Gorebeck Gaol by a man accused of rape and murder. Having been found holding the body of the last victim in his arms, the man's fate seems sealed. Nicholas is torn between a sense of duty and feelings of disgust when in the presence of the accused. Then the tables are turned, and Nicholas becomes the incarcerated . . . Duped and incensed, he swears to find the man, Wilson. But is Wilson actually guilty — or is the real culprit still to be discovered?

VALERIE HOLMES

◆

DEAD TO SIN

Complete and Unabridged

LINFORD
Leicester

First published in Great Britain

First Linford Edition
published 2014

A catalogue record for this book is available
from the British Library.

ISBN 978–1–4448–2122–2

Published by
F. A. Thorpe (Publishing)
Anstey, Leicestershire

Set by Words & Graphics Ltd.
Anstey, Leicestershire
Printed and bound in Great Britain by
T. J. International Ltd., Padstow, Cornwall

This book is printed on acid-free paper

Prologue

August 30th 1802

Nell scurried along the canal path. The cloud cover darkened the evening sky. Tonight no stars shone down to light her way. Soon what little moonlight there was would also disappear. The narrow, treacherous trail Nell followed descended precariously through roughly covered grassy banks to join the towpath that skirted the edge of the canal. She followed it along, heading towards the arch of the sandstone bridge, a short cut which would speed her way to the other side of the town, unseen. It was the last stage and worst part of her journey. Once achieved, she could climb the broken wooden steps to the higher street, where she would at last reach the relative safety of the lamplight and the outskirts of town and his house.

The water's fast flow was nothing new to her as she had traversed this route many times before, much to her mother's disapproval. As the weather closed in she was feeling the cold; her thin dress was no match for the change of season as late summer slipped into a chill autumn. Mother would be furious with her for slipping out of the farmhouse again, but that would be nothing new; she seemed to find it difficult to be anything other than vexed with her most of the time — at least when he appeared. It made Nell feel as though she was in her way, a mere obstruction to her life that should not be there. Nell stopped for a moment. Shivering, she decided it was best to complete her journey as quickly as she could. She would ask him if she might be given enough coins to buy a thicker dress from the market — or even from Cynthia Gregory's dress shop. If his mood was light, he may well say yes, at least to a secondhand one from the market. After all, he had granted her mother a new Spencer and a matching dress, so why not give her a treat too? she reasoned. A coat would be lovely, she mused, as she ventured along, her head down, picturing herself in a military-style cut coat, like his, dashing and fine.

Nell kept glancing behind her. She felt as though she was being shadowed, silent feet following her. She shook her head; this was no way for her to be. Nell was familiar with the shadows as her life had existed within them long enough; she knew their ways, yet the heaviness of her heart was causing her breath to be short and her step to be quick. She needed to make haste. When the shadows were warning you to go quickly, then only a brave man or a fool would disobey them.

He was in town tonight, but her mama had said he would be returning to London the following day. If she made it to his town house before night fell she might be able to see him one more time, without her mama being there to send her away. Nell had even thought of asking if he would take her with him. She longed to see the city, the size of the buildings, the busyness of the streets, and perhaps even a trip to a theatre or two. She even had a fancy for being an actress, but had not mentioned this to her mother — wisely.

Nell reached the stone bridge and ducked low to follow the towpath, glancing over her shoulder one last time to try and catch any sign of movement. With a sigh of relief she continued, as she saw nothing out of the ordinary. Nell bent to the stone's arched wall, ready to continue her journey into the darkness. A few minutes now from the safety of the streetlight, and from his town house. She felt her way along the wall with one hand, running it over the slime-covered curve as she stepped carefully along the ledge that served as a towpath. It was wet and often covered with mud and moss, making the going precarious at best. She was halfway there. She breathed evenly, remembering tales of goblins and ghouls that inhabited such places, told to her by an old maid — or as she called her, 'the witch', who had helped to drag her up when her mama was too busy elsewhere. Her left hand continued to inch along until the cold stone was replaced by the comparative warmth of cloth. Nell felt the rough tweed fabric of a coat beneath her fingers. For a second, her fingers explored further until she realised they had discovered another breathing form; a warm but silent entity just standing there, letting her reach out and touch, yet saying nothing. The chest was broad, rounded, and Nell smelt the man's musk mixed with the overpowering stench of ale. He stood stock-still, waiting, presumably staring toward her touch and keeping his silent vigil. Why? She let out a high-pitched squeal. Her foot slipped and his hand mercifully pulled her close to his body, saving her from a certain watery grave.

'Thank you . . . sir . . . sorry . . . ' she muttered as he held her close. It was unusual to meet someone using the path at this hour, but not impossible. She could feel the heat of his stale breath falling upon her forehead as he curled in around her, holding on firmly to her slight body. Warmth filled her cheeks as she felt his hands grip her sides, encircling her rib cage. She could feel their strength through the pitifully inadequate fabric of her dress. Like a rag doll she was flipped bodily around him and to a place of safety, her body slapped against the damp uneven stone wall. She could feel each of the bumps and grooves of the worn structure against her back, its cold surface making her shiver involuntarily — or was it something else? A growing sensation of fear? His legs straddled her small frame, pinning her there. Nell felt trapped as he leaned into her, crushing her between his heat and the cold stone.

'I'm fine now, mister. Thank you for your help. Now, please . . . Be on your way.' She swallowed. He did not move. 'I shall be fine now. I'm nearly through, aren't I? I'll be on my way home and you go on to yours, there's a good man.'

'Nell? It is Nell, isn't it?' He spoke one question, almost as a statement, his voice husky. With his hands still encircling her sides, giving them warmth, but offering no sense of comfort, she could not break free from his grip.

'Who are you, stranger?' she asked tremulously. He knew her name — how? She could not see his face, or one single feature on it, but his musk held some familiarity — or was it just the smell of gunpowder mixed with that of stale ale?

'Do you know me, sir?' she asked, her voice slightly higher than it would normally be, and louder.

'No.' His voice by contrast was low, his reply huskily brief. 'But, no worries, I soon will . . . ' His hands moved with haste. Frantically they pulled at her dress until he had inched up the muddied hem of her skirts. He breathed his fumes in short gasps onto her cheeks as his eagerness increased.

'No!' Realising his intent, Nell put the heel of her old boot against the earth and pushed as hard as she could, trying to flip him into the water, praying she could wrong-foot his bulk and offset his balance. 'Stop it, man!'

He leaned heavier into her. Nell's efforts were all futile as he yanked her skirts, bunching them up above her waist in one strong move. She gasped as the cold air found her skin, her arms pinned back by his weight, hardly able to breathe. His body pressed against hers, freeing his hands to roam at will — and he showed he had the will for them to do so. Nell tried to scream but his mouth smothered her cries. She nearly gagged with revulsion and fear. His body arched and lurched back at her, then with an unrelenting thrust, he entered her most private of places, his hands tearing the shift from her trembling flesh, exposing her nakedness.

Nell tried desperately to fight back, to wrench away, to wriggle free and move away from the pain, but all was in vain as he was stronger, bigger and determined to destroy her. His body trembled, then stilled as he groaned.

Tears welled up and flowed, ignored and dismissed by her attacker's soul, for in an instant later he had swung Nell from her perch, tossing her outside the bridge's arch and onto the grassy bank. Dampened eyes struggled to find focus through the blur. A stab of pain had shot through her as she was discarded, landing hard; it continued to hurt her side. Nell never saw the blade that he had thrust into her delicate flesh but glanced back on hearing the splash as it was tossed into the water's flow. Nell scrambled for the broken steps, and a way up to the lamplight . . . towards help, the cold air seemingly mocking her with its biting cold. Her usual balance and clear thinking had abandoned her as she swayed, half naked and fear-filled toward her destination. She felt the man's hands grasp her ankles to pull her down flat, cloying, gripping again fast at her skirt hem. She clung to the ground, her hand feeling a warm wet patch where she had fallen. The pain in her side began to sting and throb badly. Her hand found the place and Nell realised her life's blood was ebbing away.

He launched at her, one last time, but he missed his footing and slipped back, his legs falling into the canal. There was a splash as he grappled for the bank. Nell took her chance; she clawed her way to the upper path to the light, wishing she had stayed with her mother this once.

Nell made her desperate way into the town, wanting to be seen, needing now to be found and discovered even in her wretched state. She held her skirt fabric around her body to try to cover her shame and stem the flow of blood from her wound. She could see his door. With all her might she willed herself to walk or drag herself there, to find him and, in his arms, safety. If anyone could help her, he would; she knew she had only this one hope. Nell felt sorry for disobeying her mama and his orders; she should have stayed at the farm, but she so wanted a new dress.

No one followed, yet she sensed that eyes were still watching as her walk turned into a desperate crawl back to a place of safety, whilst the stranger who had climbed the bank behind her looked on from the shadow of a building and watched her die.

1

October 1802

Nicholas Penn took one last deep breath of fresh air outside the high stone walls of the Gorebeck lock-up. He glanced back at the cobbled square of the market town; wagons rattled, farmers haggled, women bartered, children's laughter melted into the animals' pitiful cries, the noise of which was in turn drowned out by the banter of the bidders. All was chaotic, all stank, yet there was colour and life here amongst the continuous whirl of people trading their wares.

A heavy lock was turned in the barrier in front of him. Nicholas breathed deeply, his broad chest glad of what fresh air there was, as his mind dreaded the prospect of seeing what he would find within the cold walls — and whom. The reinforced wooden door creaked and groaned as the warder pulled it open, grating the edge against the stone.

This journey had been, like his spirits were, very dark. He pulled the high collar of his coat close, covering the ends of his shoulder-length locks. 'Trapped sunshine', his mother had poetically described his wayward curls when he was a cosseted child. Now straighter and flaxen in hue, they had matured and grown like Nicholas himself. No sunshine would filter through behind this door. The rain started to pour down. Nicholas was silently led inside along a narrow stone corridor; he was taken further into the building's bowels, down a spiral metal staircase to an airless chasm where six bolted black doors lined the dimly lit passage. Disembodied coughs could be heard even through the iron-wood barriers which incarcerated their prey. Nicholas intuitively pulled out his kerchief and held it over his mouth. Gaol fever was to be avoided by the wise man who had the option to, but the inmates of this place had little chance to do that. The warder turned another key in the door lock at the end of the narrow corridor.

'Ten minutes!' he growled back at him.

The man had a curvature of the spine and did not look up at Nicholas's straight frame. Instead he shuffled back.

Nicholas grunted what could have been his agreement or a simple acknowledgement. The turnkey gestured for Nicholas to enter.

With some reluctance, Nicholas stepped into the small dank cell, ducking slightly so that his round hat did not contact the top of the door's stone frame. What light and fresh air there were from the open grate that served as a window, was lost to the rainwater, which now poured in, bringing with it the filth washed down from the market street above. The cell's air stank of damp and excrement. Nicholas stood equidistant from the slime-covered walls, not wanting his new riding-coat to touch anything in the place.

The cell was putrid. Under his highly polished boots was a stone-flagged floor strewn with soiled hay. Nicholas fought back memories — bleak, barefooted memories, as he glared at the figure in front of him. Like the cell, the man locked within it was unwashed, unshaven and unkempt. His appearance was in stark contrast to the man's usually immaculate presence. The figure was seated on a small stool, wrapped in a flea-infested woollen blanket, leaning against the edge of the moist wall. Even in such discomfiture he seemed to be calm in manner, resigned perhaps to his fate. Nicholas wondered if this was true. To most people in his circumstance it would have been the case, or a near breakdown of spirits, but not Wilson. Nicholas knew the man too well. He was as hard as the stone walls which held him, to the depth of the heart that beat strong within his chest.

Ebony eyes looked up at him as the door lock was slammed shut behind Nicholas, who was trying hard not to show his inner fear or his loathing of small airless spaces as much as his abhorrence for the pathetic-looking creature in front of him.

'You came, Nick!' the voice announced, louder than Nicholas had expected it to. That tone was almost as if he was annoyed at his late appearance. This was not the whispered breathy word of a dispirited soul. The confidence, the strength and the defiance were still there in his comments even if he looked to be in a physically weakened state.

Wilson's body may have been bruised, but the core of the man had not been dented. Nicholas was not sure if he felt a glimmer of admiration at the prisoner's resistance or an ice cold chill, which crept through his bones at Wilson's apparent detachment from any vestige of normal human emotion at his reduced circumstances.

'Obviously,' Nicholas replied. 'Though why, even I cannot fathom. What do you want with me? Why send for me now?' He glared back, his eyes drawn to the man opposite. 'If it is to express remorse, then I am not a priest and I do not care to hear the sordid details of your confession. So state now what it is that you want from me. This latest debacle is beneath you, sir!' Nicholas let the words slip from his lips, filled with the distaste he felt.

The man opposite sighed momentarily and then quickly coughed, covering his mouth with the back of his arm. 'Excuse me, Nick, I am not at my best.'

Nicholas regretted his harsh outburst. His inner anger had allowed him to unleash his disgust at a man who was in no position to fight back. The thought that he may have acted more like Wilson would have, had the situation been reversed, cut him deeply. 'Your appearance is wretched, man.' Nicholas needed to look away, avoid this confrontation, but what else was there to look at? The pot of slops in the corner of the room, or the rat that ran under what was supposed to be a cot? So instead, he resolved to stare defiantly back at the man.

'Who else to ask, Nick? Who else would believe in me, Nick? I am, it would appear, a damned man, even by you. You are my closest . . . '

'Please, I am not used to this tender side you show. Are you really so cowed by them . . . ?' He swung his arm around to emphasize his point. The bitterness which hung in the already suffocating air added to the sickening actual chill Nicholas sensed within the cell. It penetrated his fine coat, piercing through the lining as if

16

it was no more than a thin rag.

'Can you not speak my name, Nick?' Wilson's eyes widened as if in a gesture of humility. Nicholas knew it was false. Through the gesture those same eyes leered at him, taunting, daring, always seeking to hurt . . . to cause pain in his heart.

'Does my situation only disturb you? Does it not confound you in the slightest? I would not presume for a moment that it might upset or anger you in any way, that you might hold any true emotion for my predicament, or in fact . . . for me.' Wilson's voice trailed off.

Nicholas raised his chin. 'You'll hang for sure; most likely by the end of the month, the sentence is as good as passed. What is there for me to believe here, when a jury will not? The people want your blood, man. How have you let yourself come to this? Do you expect me to intervene with the magistrate — to appeal to him on your behalf? And on what grounds? They will gladly hang you for what you have been accused of. I could try and appeal to a higher authority, but left to the local justice, you are dead!' Nicholas stood with his boots planted evenly amongst the filth. His hands were balled black fists, the kerchief shoved back into his pocket; its resistance seemed futile. He was wearing gloves as he had no wish to touch anything in the place, lest he lose his control and wrap his fingers around the scrawny neck of the man opposite. But as that was almost certainly to be wrung legally, he had no reason to taint his own conscience with the man's blood . . . the words lingered in his mind . . . 'tainted blood'. Still, innocent until proven of guilt — was not that the way it was supposed to go?

'What they think I have done . . . I emphasize the word 'think', Nick, because you, sir, need to start to do some for yourself. 'Innocent until proven guilty', Nick. You should know that.' He raised a quizzical eyebrow in challenge.

Nick shifted uneasily. Yes, his thoughts had already taken him to those words. 'Confound it, man! You are set to be found guilty of the hideous crimes which have blighted this area in the last five months, the exact length of time you have been staying within this township, or wherever else you hole up in this region. Yet you quibble over technicalities of the law.' Nicholas drew in a long, slow breath before realising what he was doing and quickly exhaled. He composed himself and controlled his outburst. 'Are you claiming, sir, that you are really innocent?' Nicholas asked incredulously.

The man gestured to the cot. 'I am short of chairs and port, sir. But you may rest yourself upon my humble bed.' A smile cracked his gnarled face. A broken tooth showed, discoloured. He touched it with his forefinger. 'Bastards pulled off the one I got out of the mouth of a fallen Hussar. Killed the bugger myself, just for his lovely teeth, I did. He should not have bared them so readily at me; vanity, the downfall of many a good man. Took his time to go, though, amazing strength; I admired him for that. They fight on, those buggers, when there is no hope left for them. Weather was appalling too. Shame I had to relieve him of his teeth before he finally went. Still, it took his mind off the hole in his belly.' He shook his head, casting a glance at Nicholas's face as if seeking to absorb the disgust he expected to find upon it; apparently he was disappointed by the lack of response, so he continued. 'Did all that only to have some halfwit steal it at the first chance they got when they placed me in here. I tell you that there's no honour left in our world, Nick.' He shook his head, and then smiled unevenly. 'Do you have anything to eat on you?'

'My heart bleeds for you and your vanity. If that is all you sought me for, to tell me one of your charming tales of your battle 'heroics', then you have wasted both your and my time here this day, just as you have wasted your life to let it come to this.' Nicholas turned to tap on the door and summon the warder.

'They intend to hang the wrong man, Nick.' His tone was flat, devoid of wit or emotion. 'Does that answer your question satisfactorily and allay your doubts? Can you still leave knowing that is the truth of it? Will your conscience let you sleep in your crisp sheets, knowing you walked and I hung?'

Nicholas glanced over his shoulder. Wilson was standing. The blanket fell to the floor and his fashionable shirt was revealed, grubby and stained; but his back was straight, his posture perfect as you would expect a gentleman's to be.

'You expect me to believe you? You are telling me — swearing by whatever it is that you hold holy — that you did not rape and kill those girls? All five of them? Young girls! The very notion of it makes me sick!' Nicholas spat the last word out.

'Really, in some parts of the world a man can marry a young maid — what we would consider to be a child bride — and be at liberty to treat her as he saw fit, should she misbehave or displease her man, or fail to give him a son. Am I so vile, Nick? For simply liking a young maiden to dally with, as opposed to a mature wench? Tell me why this offends you so when it is in these days we allow young girls to scramble around machines doing a long day's drudge in the new mills, amongst filth and rats? Is that not a sustained daily abuse? Yet you are a prude when referring to what their body was designed for. Do you think that innocence fares well when convicted and sent to the colonies on the transports for some minor indiscretion?' The eyes of Wilson held Nicholas's, locked in a defiant stare. His words were cold, but the man's presence even when brought low was like a moth to a light. He was an enigma, a devil, and yet he projected an air of honour. 'I have told you once of my innocence in this. I shall not repeat myself again! I should have no need — not to you.'

'One wrong act or five does not make another right. Laws will change what children can legally do, and by God what can be done to them — they already are changing. In these 'foreign lands' of which you speak, I do not believe they condone abusing or killing the maids,' he sighed. 'You digress and our time here is short. They found you with the last one, holding her in your arms, her blood on you, her body half naked. If you have lied and taken me as a fool, then you deserve all you get if you are not saved. I knew you liked young wenches, not children, but . . . murder? Whoever it is that has stepped so low should rot in hell!'

'Possibly they will if such a place exists, beyond the one in which you now reside. But you do not believe it is me who murders at will, or you would not have answered my summons.' He smiled. 'Your naïvety of the world gives me my only hope that one day this place will be a better place. Despite all you have seen in Portugal and France, you still believe in honour and justice. You constantly amaze me, Nick.' Wilson's attitude relaxed.

Nicholas stiffened as the figure stepped toward him — his intense stare hypnotic, mesmerising, sickening — until he was so close that they stood, ebony eyes locking onto Nicholas's aquamarine ones.

'I met the last one — the hapless victim — yes. I knew her; she came to me — she came for me, Nick. She'd been a young wench on the cusp of womanhood: a true beauty, fresh and unspoiled, but I did not touch her in that way and neither did I kill her. She crawled to my lodgings; they followed the trail of her blood to me.' He looked away.

Nicholas sensed that there were strong

emotions being hidden deep within those cold eyes, which momentarily had moistened in an almost understandable human reaction.

However, the man blinked and the more usual cold stare returned. 'Would I, a man in my position, with my years of experience in the field, have been so careless, Nick?' His eyes bore into Nicholas's. 'Think, man. I have been a soldier who has lived behind enemy lines. I have served, done my duty and returned, yet they who do not know my past would have the world think that I would be so obvious as to hold onto a dying girl whom I had murdered, for them to find me on my own doorstep. Think, Nick. You know me; you know who I truly am. Would I be so foolishly careless? Do I look like a cold, callous murderer of innocence to you?' His voice softened. A pathetic half-smile crossed his face as he raised a quizzical brow.

Nicholas felt his gut cringe. Was Wilson toying with him? He knew the man made good points. 'Careless? No, not you. You would have covered your tracks well

enough, which is the one aspect of this affair which does not make any sense.'
Wilson nodded as if he appreciated the words as a compliment. Nicholas continued, 'Ruthless, heartless, callous, sinister . . . murdering, evil, yes! If you had a mind to. I have seen your handiwork on the battlefield firsthand, and in the villages we passed through. You forget, I know what you are capable of. What of the other girls? They bore the same trademark . . . raped, knifed, and left for dead. Are they yours, now that you can no longer kill under the guise of duty for 'King and Country'?' Nicholas tried hard to suppress a swallow, whilst he held the man's stare. He did not believe the words he was speaking but the desire to lash out at Wilson was too great; for at war, he was effective but heartless.

'Killing on a battlefield is not murder — it is for the 'greater good'. Surely you understand that. How else do you justify those that fell upon your sword?' he asked, tilting his head slightly.

'Self defence!' Nicholas answered quickly, perhaps too quickly, hiding the guilt he had felt when back in England and the memories of what he had had to do returned to him with haunting clarity on occasion.

Wilson nodded, sneering, before his manner changed abruptly again. 'The last girl was not a whore; however, she was the daughter of one, a consort. I want to find the bastard who killed her and rip his genitals out through his heart — if he has one.' The man had stopped toying with Nicholas and playing with words, and consequently Nick's emotions. Instead his message and intent were very serious, laden with a need for revenge. This, Nicholas could see, was true.

'How do you intend to do this so simply? You seem to be limited in options. Or is that why you called me here? Rather than plead your case to a higher court, you wish me to do this for you? Find this man in only a matter of days?' Nicholas said, barking back a laugh at the hypocrisy of the man and the ludicrous time restriction of the situation. If he hung for one he did not do, it still would not make him answer for all the evil he had done in the past, no matter how he tried to justify it under the guise of battle and honour. He had enjoyed taking what he wanted and celebrating being the victor. His favourite saying was *'Victori Spoilia'*: 'To the victor, the spoils'.

'No, but I needed your help, Nick. And I knew that you would answer the call of duty because you, Nick, are a man of honour.'

Nick felt the hand grab his neck. It was unexpected, quick; and as they struggled, the pincer movement of the man's fingers skilfully closed his windpipe, taking Nicholas's breath away. As his head was driven hard into the cell wall, Nicholas crumpled and fell onto the foetid ground.

Aware he was being stripped of his outer clothes, dumbfounded and dazed, he lashed out again, contacting the man's side, only to receive the final blow that would send him silently into the dimension of oblivion.

2

Nicholas left the inn and stormed through the market square. It had taken him precious minutes to regain consciousness in the cell, and even longer to raise the alarm and make the turnkey understand what had happened to him. From there it had been a travesty of slow wit and errors, as the warden could not see how an inmate could so boldly stride out of the lockup unnoticed in an ill-fitting coat and hat and brandishing a silver-topped walking stick. Nicholas could, because they were a bunch of half-wits in charge of the damned or desperate. However, their escapee had been intelligent, cold, calm and confident. His attire, his guile and his manner had blinkered them. He had been their victim, held at their mercy, but Wilson was not a man made to yield. They had seen the actions of a cornered felon in the cell and the confidence of a free man leaving, and only given a cursory glance at him, seeing what they had expected to see: a visitor leaving, in a hurry to be out in the open air again. And who would not? If only they had smelt the difference; above their own stench it might have been impossible though, Nick thought.

Meanwhile, Nicholas had been left shivering. He had been left with only his breeches, and had had to beg an old shirt in which to return to his lodgings, barefoot. For a moment he thought he was going to be charged with helping a felon escape, but the blood dripping from his hairline coupled with the bruising to his neck had helped to convince them that he had been violently attacked and was another victim of the escaped convict.

Word was sent to the local militia and to Lord Melton-Briggs, the magistrate, that a man under arrest for suspicion of being a rapist and callous murderer was once again at liberty. Meanwhile, as a futile search was ordered, Nicholas had lost precious time and Wilson had gained a head start.

With his cut now bathed, he let his hair

hang loose over the forming scab; once washed and changed, he then took to the streets in search of Colonel Wilson James Pendleton. If the authorities could not catch him, by God he would, for Nicholas had a score to settle. If they could not rid the world of the murderer, whoever the bastard was, Nicholas now had joined in the chase, and he would have to. If Wilson had any part in any of them, or was guilty of the abuse of these girls, then Nicholas swore that he would bring justice swiftly. However, it was the betrayal, the feeling of being duped, which drove him on his quest.

Two hours of covering every inch of the market town did not give up one clue as to which way Wilson had run. The community was scared of this new threat and the military presence combing the town, and so stayed close. No one would talk to Nicholas as he, too, was a stranger — as good as a foreigner to them. They did not know Nicholas, and trusted him less, because he had been in the gaol before their murderer had escaped. He had denied them the chance to see justice done for the loss of another local daughter. He sensed the hostility, driven by anger and fear. He slumped dejectedly against the stable wall and simply watched the people going about their affairs. He had to think, yet time was precious and slipping away from him.

He was now a man on a quest. What would Wilson have done? Where would he go? What if Wilson's story of the girl — the last one — was true? If Wilson was innocent of that one murder, at least, and he truly was going after the girl's murderer, then that would be where Nicholas would pick up his trail. It was a long shot; he had to convince himself that Wilson's words had not been another one of his clever lies, to cover up his tracks as he made his way to the coast to escape. What purpose would it have served though? He had already duped Nicholas into visiting him. He had seen the glint of emotion, possibly loss or grief, in his eyes. Just long enough to understand that this last victim, whoever she was, had some hold on the man. Therein lay an important link to what was left of the heart that had once been human. There was nothing for him really to be gained by denying this last and most damning murder. The others he had dismissed; but this last girl, Nell, had meant something beyond being the cause of his imprisonment. Nicholas felt a sense of pride, which he wanted to deny or at least ignore, at the thought that Wilson had turned to him for help when he was trapped. Yes, he had come and he had been duped, but how else could Wilson make sure he was safe, before an angry mob or a harried magistrate rushed through rough justice? Wilson had returned to him when he had sent for him to help — why? Loyalty? Or was it his tainted blood? His head still ached; worse still, his mind whirled with questions. More questions than answers about the man he had known for so long, and admired and despised in equal measure; yet still even now he felt as though he still did not know him properly at all.

Nicholas stopped his flow of thoughts as his skirmisher senses told him that he was being watched. He glanced along the alleyway. It was dark, quiet and still. Yet something lurked there. He had been in the services for over ten years, the last two as a rifleman; he was trained to listen and could sense danger. The life of his men and his own had depended upon his acute senses. Right now he sensed an enemy before he smelt or saw them. Nagging rebukes were cloying at his soul, for Wilson had stood before him, yet he had not realised his own danger; but the man was also a professional who had taught Nicholas much of what he knew — a bastard, but a bloody good soldier.

He caught a glimpse of movement behind an old discarded barrel and saw a small face peering out from the dirt. Nicholas casually stood up and sauntered along the passage until his shoulders were almost touching the walls of the buildings at either side.

Only inches from the barrel, the slight figure made a bold stand and stepped out of the shadows. He glanced at the narrow slit at the end of the alley where the haphazardly built buildings almost touched, as if considering making a bolt for it.

'Don't run. You have made your stand. So tell me, lad, why?'

'I . . . I . . . I know nothing . . . ' He snapped out the last word and made to run.

Nicholas grabbed the young wretch's scruff and slammed him firmly against one wall, with a little more force than he had intended to, but the lad was so slight the move had knocked the air from his lungs. The wretch kicked, punched and writhed to break free of Nicholas's grip, but his strong arm shook him again, more gently this time, just so he would cease his protest, as futile as it was. The boy did, and hung there limp and defeated in Nicholas's hold.

Nick raised the small, grubby face to his own. 'I mean you no harm, unless you raise your fist or foot to fight me once more, boy. Do that again and I shall crush you with one hand . . . Understand?' Nicholas had no intention of doing either, but the boy did not know it.

The lad nodded his head.

Slowly, Nicholas lowered him so that his feet could stand on the earth beneath them, protected by a well-worn pair of boots which looked too big for him, held on by string tied under the arch and knotted atop.

'What d'yer want of me, mister? I don't have no sister and me ma's dead and I ain't goin' to do nowt unholy in this alleyway or nowhere else.' He sniffed and wiped his nose on the back of his sleeve. The sunken eyes looked at him blankly as Nicholas took in the desperate meaning of his words.

'I am sorry about your family circumstances and I definitely do not want you to do anything of the kind. Has there been someone around here asking you for such things recently?' Nicholas asked, as he saw a fleeting look of relief in the stricken face and eyes. Nicholas knew that look, for as a child he had spent a time with his mother in the debtor's prison due to an oversight of his father's. Yes, Nicholas recognised true fear when he saw it.

'You want to get me into trouble? I ain't no dobber!' The lad looked down the alley to the bustle of the street outside.

Nicholas relaxed his expression. His brow had been permanently creased with thoughts of Wilson and his anger at the man for not having enough trust in him after all this time to tell him his plan. 'Don't even think of running or I'll hand you in at the workhouse. They always find work for idle hands, and you would be able to reach places others could not.' Nicholas leaned down to him. 'Have you ever crawled under a working loom? Big monstrous clanking beasts they are. Safe — as long as you don't get hooked up on any part that is moving. Or perhaps shovelling the cesspit would suit you even better.' Nicholas raised a quizzical eyebrow to emphasize his point.

'What do you want, mister?' The lad's voice was almost trembling.

'I want to know about the man who left the lock-up donning a round hat, carrying a cane and wearing my riding coat.' He noticed the boy's expression startle for a moment. 'You saw him, didn't you?'

The lad swallowed. He was going to shake his head.

Nicholas jangled a couple of coins in

his left hand, and smiled.

'Where is your father?' he asked, guessing he was dead like many during these times of war.

The eyes widened at the prospect of receiving a reward. 'He went with the shilling and never came back. Ma died the winter afterwards. She tried to make money for us, but instead she slowly got ill. I . . . I don't steal. I . . . ' The lad's head flopped to one side as a sob escaped him. It was then Nicholas saw the mark on his young neck. He traced his finger over it and the lad's eyes shot around, staring at him, fear making them appear to bulge to twice their normal size.

Nicholas loosened his own shirt collar to show his own bruising upon his neck. 'Where is he? Where is the one who gave you this mark?' Nicholas patted the boy's shoulder. 'He will not harm you, not whilst I am here.'

'He got you too!' The lad stared, and with a grubby finger he felt the fresh bruising on Nicholas's neck. Then he glanced up the alley, as if some malevolent force might still be watching them.

'Where is he now? Why have they not picked up his trail?'

'He had help from his woman. She got the horses from the stable yard and waited for him to come out of there. He was dressed like a real gent — like you was. You see, she had riding clobber on too. They made off toward the abbey grounds at the end of the dale. They'd be long gone by now, what with fast horses and the luck of the devil hisself with them. Those grounds are haunted, you know. The locals, and the militia included, don't go lurking there if they can avoid it cos they are filled with spirits and bad, evil . . . things . . . ' He was nodding at Nicholas as if he should know what the 'things' were. 'Evil . . . '

'That would be the last place folk would look then, because it is the last place any man in his senses would hide. However, the man I seek is capable of being evil; therefore, it would make a perfect cover for him to be in them up to his own neck; a regular home from home.' Nicholas winked at the boy, who was shivering involuntarily.

This told Nicholas where he should start looking, as Wilson had never been in his right senses and scoffed at superstition. Nicholas's young friend had seen enough evil in real life, no doubt, that if he possessed half an imagination, the tales of ghosts and demons would terrify him easily.

'How do you know all this and yet you still live?' Nicholas had let the lad loose, seeing as how they were now both Wilson's victims. 'Have you been to the abbey grounds to see them for yourself?'

The lad looked edgy and fidgeted. 'He dragged me there. Took my senses away by holdin' me throat before he was locked up. He said that how they were closing in on him and if I didn't want no apparishun following me around day and night I was to do what he told me. So I did. He told me how I had to set things right here when he was thrown in the lock-up and, if I didn't, the hounds of hell would eat me slowly, starting with me ears!' He stared into Nicholas's eyes; his fear was complete. 'The wild man let himself be caught by the river and I watched out for you like he said; when you arrived I left a sign by the end stall — a pail turned upside-down. Then this woman sought me out. She told me to watch for you; and when you was ready to go into the lock-up, I was to stand in front of the hotel and carry the pail with me. You were expected, see. It was as if he was exhausted and could not hold out till his wench arrived in town.' He sniffed and stared at Nicholas. 'So I was the link, see. But I did nowt to get him out.'

'So it was she who sent word for me to come?' Nicholas asked.

'Aye, he said word had been sent . . . Must have been the wench, because no one else knew him well enough.'

'They had this planned?' Nicholas felt as a blind or blinkered fool; a puppet who Wilson had used at will, predictable and reliable. 'Why would a woman help a murderer of young wenches?' Nicholas was doubting his initial hasty judgements; he was acknowledging the truth. Even if he wanted, in anger, to condemn Wilson, there was a greater injustice here to deal with.

'She said he was the wrong'un, and that he could not have murdered anyone at all and she knew that for sure.' The boy's voice was adamant, as if he mimicked the exact words spoken to him. 'She was not a common wench.'

A 'wrong one' perhaps would have been a fitting description for Wilson. Nicholas thought that would be accurate. 'How so? Who is she that she was so defensive of him and prepared to risk her reputation by connection with him?' Nicholas asked.

'That's all she said. I don't know who she is, but I know she loves him. You can tell — their eyes go funny — but she was more educated than most. Spoke real good, she did. Young for him though, she was — too young I would have thought, but then if he wants babies and she wants money, who knows? But he's wanted and ugly. His eyes are like holes; they don't tell no one nothin'.' He looked at Nicholas as if appraising his eyes, and shrugged in a worldly way. 'Suppose he has money. It can turn ugliness into something worth beholding, I s'pose.'

Nicholas smiled at these words of wisdom. For a young lad of limited experience, he seemed to be a thinker and mini-philosopher. 'Tell me what you see in my eyes, seeing as you are so worldly?' he said, removing his hat and scratching his aching head.

'Fire!'

Nicholas was taken aback. He had not expected such a sure response. 'Fire?'

'Yes. You are angry. They burn with anger, but your eyes also have warmth. Anyway, his didn't, only a glimmer somewhere deep down. You are full of warmth and he the chill of a snow storm, with just enough glint of sun to make the shadows even darker.'

Nicholas was not sure how to respond. He felt slightly wrong-footed by this confident declaration. There was an element of truth there, but time was passing. This was not the right place for such parlour games. Not that he thought the lad had ever been in one. 'Young?' he repeated. 'You said she was young. My age?' he asked.

'Hell, no! Young,' the lad blurted out,

but then a shadow of fear crossed his face as he realised it had not come out as perhaps he had intended. 'Not that you is old . . . ' he added.

Nicholas doubted his own judgement. The word 'young' stuck in his throat. Like the victims, would she be the next body to be found, silenced by Wilson's hand? If so, he would feel the stain of her blood on his own; the fate of this mystery woman would now be on his conscience for many a year.

'Tell me, would you recognise her again if you were to come across her?' Nicholas saw apprehension cross the lad's face.

'Aye, but they're long gone now.' He looked down. 'No good chasing them. Best let them go to someone else's patch. He'll be caught; his type always are. They get cocky, see.'

Nicholas could not help but laugh at the worldliness of his new friend's words. 'Do you have a home here? People who would miss you if you went on an adventure for a few days?'

The lad's head shot up. 'You ain't kidnapping me! I ain't going near them!'

His eyes darted along the alleyway.

Nicholas sighed. 'Don't think I would bother to ask first if I was considering kidnapping you, would I? Come with me willingly on a job — look on it as well-paid work.' Nicholas saw the apprehension lift at the prospect of earning coin.

'I told you, my family is long gone. I muck out the stables for a place to sleep, and a simple meal, but no one would miss me . . . No one!'

Nicholas ignored the pull he felt on his emotions as he sensed the loneliness and bitterness within the words. Instead, he took a coin and flicked it in the air. 'You saw me arrive here. I suspect you see a lot, young man. Therefore, you know which is my horse. Fortunately, Wilson left me that. You make it ready to go; get anything you own and wait for me here whilst I fetch my things. You and I are going on a hunting trip.' He flicked the coin to the lad, whose nimble fingers caught it mid-spin.

'Is this going to be dangerous?' he asked, feeling the coin as he moved it around his palm.

'Tell me, does your life feel safe as it is?' Nicholas asked.

The lad's face broke into a cheeky grin. 'Not particularly, not after . . . No, it don't. I am called Guy. Who are you, mister?'

'I am Mr Nicholas Penn. Call me 'sir' when in company and 'Mr Penn' when not.'

Guy nodded. Nicholas moved away.

'Mr Penn?' The voice sounded more confident already, and louder.

Nicholas stopped and glanced back.

'How do you know I won't run off with your coin?' Guy asked.

'Have you anything better to do today, Guy?'

The lad shrugged.

'I thought not. Then grab this opportunity to make a difference to your own world and the one around you, before it has passed and you starve on the street this winter. I can stop that from happening if you help.' Their eyes locked.

'What do you see in my eyes, Mr Penn?' he asked.

The word which came to Nicholas's mind was 'myself', but that would be an unwise admission, so he plucked one of the many alternatives which he could use: 'Hope.'

'I'll be waiting, Mr Penn,' Guy answered quickly.

Nicholas nodded. Instinctively, he somehow knew the lad would be fine.

3

Wilson peered out of the abandoned abbey grounds. He was famished; hunger was not something he cared for. The bastards had kicked him, thrown dirt at him. That was annoying, but never a morsel of decent food had come his way in the days he had been held in that hellhole. He had lost muscle; his normally lithe athletic body was now looking more skeletal, and his strength had been slowly diminishing, but he never doubted his call would be heard and that Nick would come as called. Just as he knew Amelia would summon him by sending his message, and she waited for him.

His heart ached, though, for his lovely Nell. Her mother, Celia, would blame him for the girl's death. She would silently grieve for her daughter, Eleanor, and hate him for not being a better father. Celia was a good wench and he knew that she would never show him her resentment openly. It was just her way, to keep her feelings hidden; he respected and understood that. It was what life had taught her to do and was the reason she had survived the Water Lanes of York as a young girl. That was where Wilson, her handsome soldier, her hero, had seen and rescued her, keeping her in a safe place and providing her with a comfortable home for their safety and of course for his own convenience.

'Thank you for the food, my dear Amelia. You did very well to organise things. I do not think that I am being unduly dramatic to admit you may have just saved my life, for what it is worth,' he said humbly.

'Please do not say that!' She rounded on him gently.

He allowed a genuine smile to cross his grizzled face. He scratched it as though it offended him. Her pale green eyes turned to him; instantly a return smile formed on those perfect lips. His beautiful Amelia, he thought. So refined . . . so perfect.

'Papa, why did we have to do it this way? Why could I not have explained to Mother the problem, and then she could have had word sent to explain who you were? Then they would have realised that they had made a terrible mistake!' Her cheeks were flushed slightly, charged with visible emotion and perplexed by the need for such subterfuge.

He stared at her for a moment — at the innocent eyes looking back at him. How had he created such a fine young woman? How had her mother kept the truth from her for so long? How had Amelia escaped from those matriarchal eyes long enough to do this daring act of bringing him one of the estate horses? She was innocent, yet some of his spirit must have slipped into her blood despite her mother's attempts to eradicate his influence from her life completely. Blood, he mused, will out. 'You know that I work for the government, my dear. Sometimes I cannot be who I really am. So I had to give them a false name, one Nicholas would recognise — 'Mr James Wilson', in this case — and I needed your help because no one would suspect your involvement in any of this. Your mama would never forgive me if I tarnished your

49

good name, Amelia, and I would die of remorse if that happened. I have only ever visited the town under the guise of Mr James Wilson. If the young woman had not sought me out, I would never have been implicated. It sadly is as simple as that, my dear. You did well to wear the bonnet; the brim shades your face well. Heavens above, your mother has enough reasons to despise me as it is without my adding this to her list of my errant ways. Although I suspect this little adventure would surpass all the other issues she may have listed upon it.' He looked at her with large puppy-dog eyes and saw hers melt as she believed his words, drinking the honeyed lies in. He actually felt a pang of guilt that he should use her so, but it was a passing emotion which he put down to his weakened state.

'Papa, if your 'work' had not taken you from us so much, I am sure Mama would think more kindly of you. Could you not come home with me now? We could hide you in the blue room until you were well enough to travel, and . . . ' She stood up, walked towards him and stared into his eyes — so direct, he thought — and so beguiling. His mind started to wander. She was so . . . perfect and genuine, with a sincerity which was beyond most of those specimens he had met of her sex. Innocence and daring wrapped into one divine package . . . too good for any man . . .

He shook his head to stop his spiralling thoughts and regain his control. 'I would not implicate either of you in my problems. You have done more than enough. Now, before you are troubled further, go back home to Mama and know you have served your countrymen well. I will clean up, change and be on my way to Whitby in no time at all. They will not find Colonel Wilson James Pendleton as easily, Amelia.' He untied the bag from the saddle, which held his clothes and a pistol from the hall. 'You did very well today, but now you need to return home. Stay close to your mother and do not venture out because there *is* a murderer at loose; and, though I may not be he, someone definitely is, and he is still at liberty.' Wilson meant his words.

She kissed his cheek lightly. 'Oh Papa, if only I could come with you.'

He tensed at her touch, fighting . . . fighting . . . always fighting those inner demons . . . fighting to regain control.

'They accused you of the murders, Father. They said they found the young girl in your arms . . . in your rented house. They described you . . . James Wilson . . . as the 'Monster', after the way the victims were brutalised. Why did she seek you out? Did she know you in some way?' There was a desperate pleading in her eyes, as if she were troubled and genuinely wanted to touch upon the truth.

It was a truth she must never discover, he thought. 'These things need not be of concern to you. I was trying to help the girl, to find out what happened to her — or who, to be more precise, had happened upon her and treated her so vilely. My efforts were too late and damned me in the process.' He saw her nod. She understood and she believed him; in a way, this time, it was true. He wanted to know which bastard had killed his Nell, his own lovely little bastard. He stared into Amelia's eyes, the same pale green as her illegitimate half-sister's had been, and almost swallowed; for his two precious girls had been similar in so many ways, yet a world apart. He had to find out who killed Nell, and why, before their trail led to his gemstone, his darling Amelia. 'Go now and not a word to a soul, you hear me? You know nothing; the government is depending upon your discretion. Now go!' He watched her nod and then mount the horse, filled with the noble resolve to do her duty for her father and her country.

'Papa, this is so unfair. You are such a good man! If only Mama could see the sacrifices you have had to make . . . ' She blew him an innocent kiss and rode off.

He sighed. Wilson watched her ride through into the forest, then reappear beyond the edge of the trees, heading across country towards the direction of the hall, returning once more to her mother's suffocating grip.

★   ★   ★

Nicholas met Guy as the boy waited behind the stable block. The innkeeper appeared as Nicholas was still a way off. He saw the man grab Guy and slap his face quite hard. The boy's gestures made it clear he was denying the tirade of accusations being launched at him by the stranger.

'Halt, man!' Nicholas shouted and quickened his step. 'What quarrel do you have with the boy?' he continued. The man froze, holding the lad in the air by the scruff of his neck. 'Guy?'

'You know him . . . sir?' the man's voice asked incredulously.

'Yes, he is working for me now,' Nicholas stated as he reached them. The boy's eyes showed gratitude as he was lowered so that his feet touched the ground once more.

'And when was you going to tell me this, eh?' He gave the lad one last shake before he let him loose.

'I tried to tell you just then but you wouldn't listen,' Guy said, and ducked as the man raised his hand; but seeing Nicholas's hand move forward, he did not complete the blow.

'I thought he was stealing away with your horse. I already was shorted for the stabling of one this morning, when this ragamuffin was supposed to be there mucking them out. I nearly set the watch on him. Thought he was in with that murdering filth what escaped.' The man's eyes looked Nicholas up and down.

'Well he is innocent of any involvement, I can assure you of that,' Nicholas said, and saw the man guffaw at the word 'innocent'. He seemed to know who Nicholas was, or at least that he was the man who had been dropped on in the gaol.

'You're a stranger here,' the man stated, eyeing him suspiciously.

'Yes. You stable my horse, therefore you know exactly who I am. Now, though, I am the man who is looking for the one who escaped. He stole my hat, coat and cane, and I want to reclaim them.' Nicholas watched the man's face, but it gave little away other than to express his disgust when Wilson was mentioned.

'Aye, you and most of the town are, whilst our women and girls hide from a monster. If he's caught they'll string him up with or without a jury for what he done to young Nell. She was a good lass, was Nell. Her ma may have been a rich man's whore, but she was pleasant enough; they both were.' He looked at Nicholas sheepishly and shrugged. 'Although you was visiting him, so did you knows him?'

Nicholas was not about to discuss his business with this wretch. He folded his arms and stared at him. The man shrugged before continuing.

'Ours not to judge, eh?' he muttered, glancing sideways at Guy.

'If it was known her mother was a consort, then tell me, was Nell treated well by all the townsfolk, especially the women here?' As he asked his question, he knew the answer already.

'Decent folk don't mix with the like of Nell and her ma, but when she was in town, I would pass the time of day with her,' he said stiffly.

'I would wager that that helped to enhance her reputation further,' Nicholas said, raising an eyebrow.

'Don't pay to judge folk!' the man

snapped, raising his chin defiantly. But hesitantly, he looked away from Nicholas's gaze. 'I run a respectable house.'

'Did Nell go in the inn often?' Nicholas asked.

'Aye, sometimes just to say hello.' He glanced around. 'She was a . . . friendly type. Not too proud like that ma of hers — not that she has owt to be proud of.' He sniffed.

'Where does Nell's mother live now?' he asked, thinking that this might be another place no one would look for the murderer of the girl. Yet, if Wilson were telling the truth, then it would be the perfect place for him to hide out — better than an abbey, under the protection of a heap of superstitious nonsense.

'She has a farm, three miles out of town. Too good for the likes of us folk,' he added, and Nicholas thought he detected a note of bitterness there. 'She has a land man, Mr Ignatius Granger, who lives on the edge of the land in his own cottage. He runs it for her. Some say he does more than that for her, but you know how tongues wag.' He winked. 'She visits the town when she needs or wants to. She is kept well by her 'benefactor'. But Nell wandered off more freely. I think she found it lonely out there, and so liked to walk into town often. The mother prefers her own company.' He shrugged. 'No doubt had too much of other sorts before, eh? Now where will Nell walk, or will her spirit roam freely as the lass did? It will be a brave man who walks the canal path on a night from now on.' He shivered, genuinely paled by the notion.

Guy stepped behind Nicholas, obviously frightened at the thought.

'Come on,' Nicholas said, as he lifted the boy on top of the horse. He nodded to Silas Mann before leaving.

The innkeeper folded his arms and watched them ride away, his face still set in a grimace.

Nicholas glanced back, doffed his hat and rode off. A gnawing thought ate at his mind — Nell's father was a wealthy man. Could it be — ?

4

Sarah-Beth hated her life at the big house. She looked down at her once-soft hands, their skin all reddened and rough. It had seemed such a grand idea to be working in a manor house, known locally as the Hall, grand with its own farmland, where she would see equally grand people — watch how the nobility lived. See how a lady really acts when she receives visitors. It was to have been the start of her future, like a new beginning in life. Somehow, Sarah-Beth always knew she was going to improve her position.

* * *

She sighed at those dreams, of being able to marry a butler or a gamekeeper. Someone who would treat her well and provide her with everything she needed to have a fine family. However, dreams sometimes fade when they are exposed to reality; the butler here was almost retired. The housekeeper hated her with a passion, or so it seemed to Sarah-Beth — jealous no doubt of her young looks, she reasoned — and the gamekeeper was already married, although his eyes were keen to watch her whenever he had a chance to. She smiled at the way he did, but never when his wife was around. There were no males in the family for her to woo; no one in the inner circle of the household 'court' for her to use her womanly ways on to provide her with her own rooms, like Prinny did with his 'ladies' if the gossip from the inn was to be believed. Nope, here only the stable-lad was young enough to be with her, but his was not the brightest brain in the stable and that included those inside the heads of the horses he tended. She smiled at that thought.

At the start of laundry day she had felt fine, knowing that by the end of it she would feel as though her back would break from lugging her sodden burdens about from soaking tub, to wash tub, to scrubbing board, and finally to rinse before wringing and mangling. Stretch, hang, press or starch, it was an unrelenting list of chores for one slight wench to do who was light of frame and quite short in stature. In not so many years from now her skin would peel off her tiny fingers and her cheeks would show the red hue of broken veins.

Sarah-Beth also hated the early morning starts, getting up before the sun, listening to birds singing their songs as if they were filled with happiness; it just did not feel natural to her. The heat from the water and the lye irritated her skin and, before she was much older, she knew her beauty would be ruined by the steam and the long hours of drudgery. Sarah-Beth had no intention of letting that happen to her. She would find a way out of her hole and use her looks as a passage to a better life, whilst she still had her maidenly freshness.

She carried her heavy load in her wicker basket out to the washing green, over which was stretched the long lines. If the clouds stayed away here she would be able to spread the sodden cloth, to air off the results of her labours. She held the young miss's bed linen up and, as her eyes focused on the distance, she noticed a stranger watching her from the corner of the field. The sunlight was behind him, giving his shape an indistinct edge as she squinted, trying to make out the figure's detail. He was quite tall and looked to be wearing a fine coat and round hat. Sarah-Beth continued in her task, yet watched him with great interest and saw him lean against yonder fence, folding his arms casually in front of his chest as if admiring the view — of her. He seemed in no hurry to move. She smiled.

To stare back would be forward of her. Sarah-Beth knew enough of manners not to look that common, and neither did she want to appear as a desperate maidservant, so she decided upon a more restrained approach — one which would keep his eye trained upon her. To ignore him would be the right thing to do. If he had wanted her to announce his presence as a visitor, then he would have followed the path to the hall. So Sarah-Beth continued hanging each piece of fabric on the line as if she was the picture of perfection personified. She stood with a straight back, held her head high and chin up, and paused for a moment to look up to the sunlight and adjust her bonnet, releasing a wayward curl or two as she did. Then she removed it, shaking her voluminous hair out, before sweeping it back up into its confined uniform of her cloth work-bonnet. She bent low, extending her arms to show her clear line, and continued to work.

When her last sheet was straddled over the line and had been smoothed down, she glanced back at where the stranger had been standing, but to her disappointment he had gone. She sighed and looked down at her empty basket. She stared at the ground and sighed again. An empty basket sums up me life, she thought. She would have to dream on, her notions keeping her entertained as she imagined living in such a house as its mistress. No handsome stranger was going to appear and whisk her away today. But as she thought those words, a pair of boots came into her eyeline behind the bottom of the last sheet she had hung. She stepped back.

His head appeared around the edge of the fabric, a wry smile on the familiar face that gave her a cheeky wink, followed by a gentle nod toward the old stable-block.

'You!' she exclaimed.

He put a finger to his lips and gestured more determinedly to the old buildings behind the manor house.

'Why are you here, and what on earth are you dressed like that for?' she asked as he casually strode away.

He turned slightly, beckoned to her with his index finger, as he took a step backwards. Then he turned, smiling, and still gesturing that she should be quiet, as he deftly made his way to the shelter of the unused building.

Sarah-Beth knew too well what he wanted. She glanced toward the manor house and then to her empty basket. A good job done! she thought to herself. No one should be up at this hour. Miss Amelia would be still abed, as would her mama. They slept half their life away; and the mister, well, he'd left 'em long ago. No wonder the mistress seemed to be such a frigid old bat. Sarah-Beth smiled. Well, she thought, as she quickened her step, a girl was only young once; and besides, for what he wanted, there would be no way a baby would be made. Besides, he gave her good coin; she would have a new bonnet by Christmas at this rate.

Sarah-Beth hid the basket behind the log-pile and answered his summons. 'One man is as good as another,' she whispered, stifling a laugh at her own private joke. She wiped her mouth on the back of her hand and grinned.

What Sarah-Beth did not know was that her initial wish was about to be granted — she would never see her hands turn rough again, or her skin peel off, or her cheeks made ruddy by steam, or her back made permanently bent by years of bearing heavy burdens. This man would indeed see that she would never age before her time, for death would stop her youth in its tracks.

5

Nicholas Penn left the market town, glad to leave the grim memories of it behind him for now. He had his rifle with him. It would now stay with him, like an old friend, giving him the feel that he was once more on a mission. He had lost his gentleman's riding coat to Wilson and now donned his caped Garrick greatcoat. The boy nestled on the saddle behind him. He had managed to find a better pair of children's boots for the lad's frozen feet on a stall of cast-off clothing in the market, which fitted comfortably enough. He had no reason to be charitable and his mood was not in the right frame for such acts, but he saw Guy's plight and had overlaid his own childhood feelings of being cold as they had languished as a family in the debtor's gaol until his father had finally managed to bail his mother, baby sister and self out. Too late for his mother's health, as the fever had got to her and then took the baby too. That was then and, as he peered ahead along the moorland path, this was now.

He followed the track to the farmhouse at the end of a lonely country lane that was surrounded by the beauty but harshness of the moorland expanse. Behind him their path veered off through a narrow forested stretch of land to the vale where the town lay. He could not help but think about the lonely journey the young woman had made, frequently apparently, if Silas Mann the innkeeper was to be believed. And for what reason? To be frowned upon or spurned by the respectable townsfolk? Yet, she had decided to make this vigil on her own. Not just to talk to the innkeeper, surely? He was a man of means, relatively, but he doubted that Silas Mann was as harmless as he had tried to portray himself to be. So why did she go to seek out Wilson? Why go along a deserted canal path? Unless she did not want to be seen walking out on her own by the already hostile townsfolk? The same people who now indignantly sought revenge for the grievous wrong committed against a vulnerable young wench. His gut churned at one obvious thought: Wilson's seal was deeply etched in this, but in what way? He remembered the glimmer of raw pain shown in the man's usually impenetrable gaze when he spoke of this woman . . . Why?

The house where Nell's mother lived looked to be in a good state of repair. One woman had definitely not maintained it so without help, muscle and the means to have the necessary jobs done. The groundsman, Granger, was nowhere to be seen. The cottage was the other side of the forested path. Nicholas glanced around but there was no sign of movement in the outbuildings. Nicholas paused, watched and listened. This would be no easy visit, but where else was there for him to go to find the missing man? In the abbey grounds? A wild goose chase, he decided. Wilson was too competent a soldier, Nicholas reasoned — or had been, to leave such an easy trail for him to follow. He would not want to face Nicholas's fury without being better prepared. Wilson would let his anger cool down before he would be found. He had left him in the gaol, not in an open or desolate place. However, there had been no certainty that Nicholas would not be beaten, threatened or incarcerated himself. Wilson had betrayed what bond they still had left between them.

The boy bounced around on the horse; having never ridden before, he seemingly enjoyed the newfound freedom. His head darted from side to side as if the world beyond the town was a new revelation to him.

'Guy, I want you to hold the horse when I dismount. I will knock upon the door. You cough once if it is the same woman who comes out, the one that you saw in the town. I suspect she may have a connection to Wilson. If I am wrong, then we will soon know, for a woman who has just had her daughter callously murdered will be baying for somebody's blood, unless she has had her heart broken beyond repair. In either case, I suspect that this visit will be short.' Nicholas winked at Guy, trying to reassure him.

'Long as it's not our blood, eh, Mr Penn?' The lad chuckled.

Nicholas smiled at the comment. However, losing people was no cause for humour, and the lad should already have discovered the truth of that. He walked the horse to a fence opposite the farmhouse door. There he dismounted and handed the reins over to Guy. 'Cough just once if it is she you saw at the stables. Or stay silent if not, but keep watch and shout if you should see any sign of the groundsman. His name is Granger.' Nicholas strode toward the door. He thought he saw a drape move in the corner of the small window to the right-hand-side ground floor window.

Nicholas lifted and then clanged the heavy door knocker, letting it fall loudly against the brass. He waited. No response. The curtains did not move again. He lifted it once more. 'CLANG', but still no one came. His plan was not working. She must be in, he reasoned; someone was definitely there, of that he was certain. That curtain had moved, and not by a supernatural force. He gestured to the lad to stay with the horse. 'If I whistle once, bring the animal straight away.'

The lad nodded. He looked more excited than scared. With wide eyes he stared at everything around him, taking in all the details and, as he had been entrusted to do, watching, covering Nicholas's back.

Nicholas ventured around the side of the building. If no one would come to the door, then he would find a way inside. If Wilson was there, he would seek him out. If he wasn't . . . well, then he would decide what to do and say if he was faced with a distraught and frightened woman. First he needed to see her, or at least to let Guy see her.

He traversed the ground around the farmhouse, looking for any sign of life, his senses keen to pick up on anyone watching him. There were two horses stabled, but both were solidly built and quite old, as though they were more used to pulling a plough than a carriage, or being seated upon by a lady of any rank at all.

Nicholas left the stable and turned

toward the farmhouse, seeing a glow of lamplight from the back windows. The door to the scullery had been left wide open. Standing to the side, he peered in, then strode purposefully along the stone-flagged corridor, approaching an open archway through which he could see the kitchen range and the dairy beyond.

As quick as a spark from a tinder box he moved, ducking a broom handle as it was swung at his head. He caught it with his right hand and dragged the perpetrator of the near-devastating strike with it, swinging them around into the full grip of his arms. The woman was slight of figure, wearing the apron of her position. She swore like a trooper, threatening him with everything from the birch, to castration, to the gibbet upon the moors. Using his height and superior strength, he lifted her off the floor and spun her to the wall, clamping his hand across her mouth. She yelped like a scared puppy, once loudly, before he managed to silence her.

'Still yourself, woman! I mean you no harm. No one answered the front door. I merely wish to see your mistress,' he said as calmly as he could, trying to still her fear as he would a nervous horse, his voice almost whispering. Terrified watery eyes stared back at him, blinking frantically. Her body stilled though.

Nicholas repeated his message with a little more surety. 'I want to see your mistress. Calm yourself now. Do you understand that I do not wish you any harm?' He slowly let her down and released the hand from her face. His rifle was still slung over his shoulder.

She drew in a sharp breath. 'She is in mourning. You is not to see her. She will not see anyone.' The woman was visibly shaking. 'I thought you was . . . him, the . . . '

'Enough, Ellie!' a woman's voice shouted along the corridor to them.

Nicholas looked to its owner. He saw her clearly: the striking figure of a woman in her early middle years, still very attractive and well-groomed, standing with a straight back, and completely dressed in black, from neck to lace-gloved hands. She held her head high, and pointed a regulation rifle directly at him. This, at least partially, suggested there was a connection between Wilson and this woman. He had come to the right place, not the shadows of a deserted abbey.

Nicholas stood back and faced the woman squarely. The maid ran behind her mistress.

'Who are you to disturb my house at such a time as this? Do you not know we are in mourning, sir?' Her voice was steady. Her hand did not waver; and her manner, although not calm, was certainly controlled.

'My apologies,' Nicholas answered. Her voice, he thought, sounded educated, although there was still an underlying local twang to the way she pronounced her vowels. A curious mixture, he thought, for a wench in deep mourning. Her hand, thankfully, was steady upon the trigger. He either admired her resolve or wondered how close she had actually been to the daughter she now mourned. 'May I speak to you, please? I am looking for him, and I think you may be able to help me in my search.' His question was deliberately obtuse.

She lowered the rifle, still holding it firmly across her body, then turned slightly and nodded to her maid. 'Fetch a tray and bring it into the day-room.' She glanced back at Nicholas.

The maid, Ellie, paused; but one determined gesture from her mistress sent her scurrying into the kitchen.

Nicholas stepped forward, and immediately the gun was aimed at its target. 'There is a boy standing outside the front of my home, sir. Who is he and why is he there?'

Nicholas thought it was interesting that she had not queried who it was that he sought. Did she know he was chasing Wilson, or did she presume he was hunting the murderer? Either way, it looked like he would be welcomed into her home soon. 'He is tending the horse. He is a waif who was in the town and needed help — a home.'

Her features were set hard. 'You need a boy to tend a horse? Why not leave the boy at your stables?' she asked.

'Where is he?' Nicholas asked, ignoring her comment.

She stepped back into the archway of the kitchen. 'Go through to the room at the end of the corridor — and no tricks, or I will fire and the devil will take you. For I will say you entered here armed and attacked my maid. Who will find me guilty of anything but my own defence, after what has been done to my Eleanor?' She gestured with the barrel of the gun for him to start walking.

He strode purposefully through the distant door which led into the main part of the house, crossing a narrower corridor which served as an entrance hall. The home was warm, but not spacious in the way a manor house was. Functional, he thought, rather than elegant. However, Nell, he realised, had a grander title: 'Eleanor', yet she ran around the town like a wench of the night.

The woman pointed with the rifle to the large wooden door to his right. Nicholas pushed it open, looking carefully through the gap as it broadened, revealing a parlour of sorts. He stepped inside, moving a heavy piece of fabric which was obscuring the door from opening to its fullest. The doorway had been hung with a heavy velvet curtain, no doubt to keep out the draughts. Inside the room a fire burned low in the grate; it was badly in need of stacking and stoking.

Once inside, he stood by the mantel-shelf and, as he bent to poke the coals below the low flame with the iron poker, he saw that a well-used pipe had been propped at the end, a leather pouch of tobacco tucked at the side of a worn leather wing chair.

The woman followed him in. Cautiously, she remained standing with the door behind her and lowered the rifle slightly again. 'Sit if you wish, but don't make yourself too comfortable, for you will have your drink and leave, once you have paid your respects.' She spoke without any hint of feeling.

Nicholas thought she had the same detachment from emotions that Wilson showed. They would make a fine pair. Nicholas could have disarmed her in two movements, but he knew that he did not need to. 'Where is he?' Nicholas repeated.

'The murdering bastard who took my

baby's life?' she said, again almost devoid of emotion, despite the hatred that the woman displayed within her words. 'Or the man who knocked you senseless, Mr Penn, and left you to pick up his pieces?' She stared at him with eyes which he could see burned with anger, fury and betrayal. 'You have done well to find your way here, sir, so soon.'

'Both!' he said. 'I want to know where both are.'

Nicholas watched her pale blue eyes as they gazed beyond and behind him, to the window where the curtain had moved earlier.

6

Nicholas turned around slowly. A figure emerged from behind the curtain, cleaner than when his eyes had last fallen upon him, and dressed in the travel attire of a gentleman of the city — attire which fitted perfectly, as it was made for him by his tailor in St James, London. He stood there, as bold as brass, donning a top hat and holding a silver-topped cane — Nicholas's.

'Give me one good reason, sir, why I should not take that cane and beat you till your bones crack?' Nicholas greeted his ex-senior officer with the respect he felt he deserved.

Wilson gestured with the cane, his arms wide, as if in resignation. 'I can understand your anger, Nick.'

'You asked me for my help, then stole the clothes from my back and left me amongst your stench and detritus!' Nicholas spoke out, seeing the woman raise the rifle higher again, training the sights on him. His voice was even but the intensity within his words was unmistakable. 'They nearly sent me to York Assizes as your accomplice! Tell me, would you have come so readily to rescue me if they had?' Nicholas glanced at the woman; she was starting to annoy him.

Wilson gestured with the stick that she should abandon the gun. 'Of course I would. How else, Nick, was I supposed to leave the establishment when they were obviously enjoying my company so much?' He smiled, revealing that he had replaced his missing tooth. His smile grew as Nicholas's eyes could not help but look upon it. 'I asked the man to give it back to me when he left the establishment, Nick, later that same day. He never thought I would stay around to reclaim it. Do not worry; his sorry being still breathes, somewhere.' Wilson shrugged as if the man's fate was of no consequence to him.

'You trusted me to come to you when you asked for me to. Could you not trust me to help you further? Did you have to leave my being in peril of being locked up as an accomplice to you? Did that possibility not cross your mind?' He had raised his voice unintentionally.

'It was safer for you, that I did not. It looked more genuine the way it happened, as an unsuspecting attack upon a do-gooder. Please, do not raise your voice here, for there is a lady present, and one who grieves the loss of her daughter. That same daughter who lays next door, waiting to find her own peace. She will be at rest tomorrow and I would have you there representing me and at my good friend's side.' He stepped away from the window and stood beside the woman, removing the rifle and guiding her to the high-backed chair next to the fire. She moved as if devoid of any feeling; a functioning shell: no warm response to his touch or any noticeable rejection of it. Nicholas wondered what scene he was witnessing, for Wilson himself had his eyes focused upon the woman with what he could only describe as consideration or tenderness. Nicholas did not speak as his emotions raged within him. He, in part, wanted to run at the man; yet, it seemed equally appropriate that he keep his silence and wait for the next part of this cameo to be played out.

When the lady was seated, Wilson looked at him squarely. 'Your clothes will be found discarded by the river in the grounds of the abbey. I could hardly give them back to you without suspicion falling upon your broad shoulders once again, and they are very unpleasant in the way they ask their questions in that place.' He half-smiled. 'Can't take it themselves, though.'

Nicholas looked at the woman. 'What hold does this man have over you? Speak freely, ma'am, for I am here and will not let further harm come to you.' Nicholas watched her face lift. Wilson stood idly behind the chair, expressionless. Nicholas had tried to take all trace of anger from his voice as he spoke to her.

'Sir, there is no more harm that can be done to me, is there? The girl that I bore, my only child, whose existence tied me to this man, is no more. She is destroyed, as is my life. I now have no purpose here. I must leave and take with me the memories and lost years of my existence. What more can you do to me, sir, that has not already been done?' She cast a casual, yet pointed glance at Wilson, who placed a hand upon her shoulder, almost stroking it with his palm.

If this woman was said to be a whore, as the innkeeper had described her — a kept woman — she was nothing like the image of one that had been conjured up within Nicholas's mind. Her grief appeared to be genuine, but was seemingly more for her own plight than for the dead daughter who was laid out in the room next to them. No wonder Nell had so often taken herself off from this house and ventured into the town.

'Explain this madness, sir!' Nicholas's words were sharp.

Wilson nodded. 'Eleanor, my dear spirited little Nell, was my daughter.'

Nicholas swallowed, although why this should cause him any pain he had no notion; for Wilson had done far worse in his lifetime than raise an illegitimate child. However, Nicholas now understood why Wilson had shown a trace of genuine emotion. He had apparently loved the child as his daughter. 'What of Amelia?' Nicholas could not stop himself from asking about the daughter he knew about, the rightful one who lived in a manor house, the Hall, not so many miles from this very place, with her own doting mother.

'What of her? She lives, she is healthy, and Nell looked amazingly like her. Neither she nor her mother know of the existence of the poor girl, and as for the matter of my friendship with Celia, I believe the mother . . . '

'Can you not speak your wife's name in my presence, sir?' Nicholas was incredulous that the man could have so many parts to his life, yet remain detached from them in this cold-minded manner. He felt for the woman, Celia, as she sat there listening to this.

He raised a hand to silence Nicholas. 'Do not interrupt if you wish to know the truth of this situation, and do not lecture me on my affairs. That 'woman' knows of this dear lady's existence and has done for a number of years, but she is ignorant of whom it was that I found comfort with or that I had another child here.'

The lady's cheeks flushed slightly as she looked boldly into Nicholas's eyes.

'My dear Nell was a joy to me,' continued Wilson, 'a gift of that friendship — a special gift. Where Amelia is shallow like her mama — delicate, perfect in many ways, and kept away from me by her mother's design — Nell had grit and character, which unfortunately left her vulnerable. I have kept my affairs quiet from the world. I have a man on this estate who has watched over their safety and who owes me deeply. Therefore, I am aggrieved that when Nell needed me, it was too late for me to help her and she had slipped out beyond his reach — a fact I have stressed to him in a manner that he will forever remember.' He stared at Nicholas. 'She died in my arms — and yes, you might be ready to charge me with the fact that others have died by my hands, but that was war. This is here and now, and I will have the bastard's gullet ripped from his begging throat when we find him, Nick. Because find him we will!'

He breathed deeply and composed himself. 'I apologise, my dear, for the outburst.' Wilson looked up, breathed deeply again, and when his eyes focused once more upon Nicholas, they had had their cool indifference restored.

The lady's back had stiffened. She nodded to acknowledge the apology. There was a knock at the door. The woman stood and Wilson took his position behind the curtain, before the maid was allowed in. Nicholas had seated himself opposite the fire, looking at the lady who waited for the maid to leave before Wilson returned to them.

He helped himself to the fresh parkin which was laid out on a fine plate. He seated himself on what was obviously his favourite worn gentleman's chair and crossed his legs casually as he ate.

'We?' Nicholas remarked. 'You said 'we'.'

'Nicholas, tomorrow morning I need you to attend the ceremony with Celia here, alias Mrs Trent. Watch out for anyone in the crowd who will gather as the cart takes her and Nell through the town to the church yard. My man, Ignatius Granger, will be there at the back, sombrely attired, but with the eyes of a hawk; as he, too, was a skirmisher who has sussed out many an enemy behind the lines. After the burial service he will escort Celia to an address in Harrogate . . . '

'Harrogate!' She said the word as if rolling it around in her mouth, and her eyes showed life for the first time — animation, and a flicker of hope. She actually dared to raise the corners of her mouth into a vague smile.

Nicholas was amazed as years seemed to instantly peel away from her troubled face.

'Yes, my dear Celia. You have been in 'exile' here long enough. Your home will be an address in Harrogate now, and a wardrobe will be made ready for you. I will attend you there when my business here is done, and we may part as friends. Pack only a small bag, for this move will be discreet. Nicholas and I will need this place to use as our base. Take the maid with you. She has no family here and her man is at war.' Wilson looked to Nicholas after he had despatched his latest orders and just changed the two women's lives in one announcement. Celia was obviously at his mercy and completely under his control. Any thought of his generosity was stifled within Nicholas, as she had not been given her freedom, had she? But merely moved from one place of incarceration to another. The rooms might be better tended than the cells in the lock-up, but freedom was something which was not in Wilson's offer. However, the woman seemed to be impressed by his arrangements.

Celia Trent turned to Wilson and hugged him tightly with genuine enthusiasm that openly showed she was still a young woman at heart. 'Excuse me,' she said sweetly. 'I must tell the maid and attend to my things. We have much to arrange for tomorrow and beyond.' She left with what Nicholas could only describe as a lighter mood and step.

Both men looked at each other.

'She grieves deeply,' Nicholas commented dryly.

'She was no more than twelve when she found herself with child.'

Nicholas shook his head. 'Could you not control your appetite, man?'

Wilson shrugged. 'Do not judge. She was a very forward and well-developed young wench, spoilt and available, and I was being forced by Father to marry a woman with as much passion in her blood as the girl next door has now. I loved Celia on sight — still do — but she gave me Nell, and now some bastard has taken her and I want him found. Celia will be safe and will have all the things having the child took away from her. I will return to her when my business is done; but Nick, we have a murderer to catch before he can get anywhere near my Amelia. Unless you could live with that thought, I need you to attend the funeral tomorrow. I will watch from the shadows. He will make a mistake, for he is a cocky bastard, this man. He would dare to kill my child within spitting range of my home.' Wilson's hand was balled, but hung by his side.

'You are assuming that he knew who you were and what relationship you had to the girl. Are you forgetting the other murders? Are you forgetting that more lives than Nell's have been lost at his hand and that he may have long since left this place?' Nicholas was keeping his voice calm, but he did not feel so himself. The thought that this man could so easily justify his double life galled him.

'No! I have not forgotten anything, Nick. Two of these girls I visited in Harrogate, and one in Whitby. He dogs my heels like a wolf — nay, a spirit. If he was a wolf I would have had its pelt by now and stuck the head upon the wall. He knows me — in some way. He stalks my haunts. He kills the girls that I would treat well and reward for the favours they have served me with.'

Nicholas stared at the flames. 'The favours of sin.'

'Call it what you will, Nick. I have never treated one badly, and often saved them from the worse fate of starving. Call it 'sin' if you feel so raised above such base acts, but those three girls and my Nell are dead to it now. Their lives have been taken and he — whoever he is — has destroyed them first, before ending their existence in this world. Help me to find him, Nick, before he takes my Amelia! When Celia goes to Harrogate, I would have you go to Amelia and make sure she is safe. She will trust you.'

'Was it Amelia who brought the horse?' Nicholas's eyebrows rose at this obvious solution to his problem. Who else could have got word to Nicholas? But to risk her so . . . surely not even Wilson would do that.

'Yes. Forgive me that one error of judgement, but I had so little time, and I knew that they would hang me. Then no one would know the truth of it, which would leave Amelia even more exposed, as the hunt for a murderer would have ceased.'

Nicholas could not forgive him anything at this point. He managed always to excuse whatever dismal act he had committed to suit his own ends. 'Your wife — will she welcome me with a warm heart?' Nicholas asked, and he saw the usual dark shadow fall across Wilson's eyes at her mention. 'I thought not.'

'Avoid her if you can, or go boldly to

the front doors — the choice is yours. If she knows they are in danger, she will bend her pride to allow you into her home. But how you will stop her involving the militia and the over-stuffed buffoon Melton-Briggs . . . He would love to move for her and discredit me. If he had realised who it was that was to be brought before him at the assizes under an alias . . . well, he would have speeded my demise before my true identity could have been revealed.'

'Exactly, Wilson. You have so many enemies, and it is now her home! She may well have me thrown off the land.' Nicholas stared at the man, loathing, respecting, pitying — a whole tumult of emotions all mixed, all confused and all fighting to bury the one true emotion he had subdued from the day he was sent away to school at the age of seven, never to return: rage.

Wilson ignored his comment. 'Will you help me? I will not ask again. If you want no part of this, then go now and take that scrap of humanity who lingers outside with you.'

Nicholas had almost forgotten about Guy, who would be patiently waiting with the animals.

'I will help you, for Amelia's sake. I have no wish to add her fate to my conscience, if anyone should hurt her. I will do that for her, and for the lives you have tainted — and, perhaps indirectly, caused the murder of by association.'

Wilson nodded and stared at him, a look of surprise showing subtly as if he had not connected any blame to himself at all. 'Will you not do it just because I have asked you, Nicholas?' Wilson asked quietly.

Nicholas looked at him momentarily as he registered that his formal name had been used. He did not answer his question. 'I will be here tomorrow to act as escort.' He left.

7

'I thought you had decided to stay here the whole night.' Guy held out the horse's reins. His hand was shaking and Nicholas realised that he looked quite cold.

'Here, see if this makes it worthwhile.' Nicholas offered him a slice of the freshly baked parkin.

The boy's eyes lit up and he took the food and let go of the reins, eating it greedily — or, more accurately, hungrily. Fortunately, Nicholas caught the leather strap and steadied the horse. Meanwhile, Guy ate it as if he was starving. That was when Nicholas realised that his interfering in this boy's life had left him with another problem. He deftly swung into the saddle and then reached out a hand and plucked the problem up, seating him in front of him. Nicholas swung the rifle from his back and slipped it into the saddle holster.

'Where are we going now, mister?' Guy

asked, finishing the last crumb which had fallen onto his sleeve.

'Mister Penn!'

The shout took them both by surprise. Ellie the maid was scurrying around the edge of the building and waving at them with a piece of cloth. Nicholas steadied the spooked horse. She stopped waving erratically and stood still whilst Nicholas walked the horse over to her.

'What is it?' Nicholas asked.

'The mistress says as you can let the lad sleep in the kitchen by the fire, whilst you goes about your business.' She smiled at Guy. 'I think I could find him summit to eat,' she said warmly.

The lad was already sliding off the horse; he needed no second invitation. 'Very well,' Nicholas said.

The woman put a hand on the boy's shoulder as he ran enthusiastically over to her. Nicholas could see an expression of delight in the lad's eyes as he glanced back. How long had it been since Guy had been cared for properly by his mother? Too long, he thought; that was obvious. Then Nicholas glanced at the woman whose expression was not so gentle when she looked at him. 'I am sorry about the earlier misunderstanding, Ellie. I hope I did not scare you.'

She held her head high. 'You did!'

'He's a good man, miss,' said Guy.

'That's as may be, but it don't do to go bursting in on folks' houses, not at a time like this.' Her eyes were watery. 'Not at any time really, not like that.' Nicholas realised she was feeling the shock and grief that he would have expected to see displayed by the mother. This woman at least had been fond of Nell. 'However, what's done is done and I knows you weren't acting out of menace, so I accept your apologies as they are intended.' She nodded at him as if to stress her point.

Nicholas did likewise and turned the horse around ready to ride away, when another rider appeared at full gallop, heading toward the farm across the open field. Nicholas pulled out the rifle. 'Go inside!' he snapped to the woman and boy.

'No, mister, don't shoot him. That is Mr Granger. If he is riding like that then summut bad's up!' Ellie shouted, panic audible.

Granger reined in as he reached the farm. He ignored Nicholas's presence completely, dismounted practically before the horse stopped and strode at a pace inside. Nicholas did likewise, with Ellie and Guy following on behind.

Wilson had obviously been watching the man approach from the window and was standing in the entrance hall waiting for the news. 'What gives, Granger?' he snapped.

'There's been another one, sir. Over at the Hall.' The man paused as his words sank in.

'Amelia?' Wilson's face paled.

'No, sir, she is safe. Her mother has been taken along with her, under the armed escort of Lord Melton-Briggs, to his estate. The girl was their maid, Sarah-Beth Jenner. Same done to her as Nell.' He removed his hat and held it before him.

Ellie gasped. Her hand shot to her mouth whilst her other curled around Guy's shoulder, pulling him in to her.

Wilson stared at Granger; he seemed momentarily dumbstruck.

Nicholas gestured to the maid that she should take Guy to the kitchens. 'Lock the doors. Don't leave access to the building open anywhere: check for open ground floor windows, hatches and cellars. Ellie, be quick and carry a knife on you. Guy, you help her all you can.' She nodded, holding Guy's hand firmly in hers. At least, Nicholas thought, they would be solace for each other for one night.

'Damnation! We must catch this man whoever he is!' Wilson snapped out the order, exploding his words like a volley into the silence which had surrounded them again.

'Sir,' Granger continued, 'you need to go to ground. They are hunting you with a vengeance and will not stop until they have your blood. They found the hat which you wore to escape from the lock-up by the body, and therefore the murderer they are still seeking is you — in their eyes, for definite. You'd be shot on sight or lynched if they recognised you.'

Wilson sat on the bottom stair opposite the doorway, his head in his hands, and rubbed his eyes with the ball of his palms. Ruffled by events, he looked up. 'They will never suspect that I am here, but I will have to hide in the loft space tomorrow for the duration of the gathering. It will not be safe for me to look on. Granger, you have done well. Go with Celia and be her shadow the moment the service has concluded. The world will think she has been holed up here, a recluse locked away with her grief. Ellie will now have to stay here to keep up the appearance of normality. Find Celia a reliable maid in Harrogate. You know the type: young, able, but simple enough to do as she is told without question. You choose her, not Celia. Vet her. Nicholas, tomorrow you must be my eyes and ears. I need you more now than I ever have in my life.' He stared up at Nicholas.

Nicholas could not help but raise a quizzical eyebrow. It was the first time he had heard the man admit that he needed him at all, or ever had. It touched Nicholas despite his best efforts to remain detached: Wilson was hurting; he had an invisible enemy dogging his tracks and threatening the previously successful duality of his domestic world. Even now, though, he saw a flicker of a smile on Wilson's lips as he acknowledged he had managed to truly shock Nicholas with his chance admission.

'I will keep watch. You two both need sleep tonight because you will have little time for it from tomorrow onwards until this bastard is caught. He knows who I am. Even if those fools at the gaol chase an alias, this blackguard knows exactly where to find my family estate. Once my Nell is buried, Granger, you will be needed to keep a close eye on Celia and look after her well in Harrogate. Meanwhile, you and I, Nick, are going to flush out a species of rank vermin.'

8

The church had been almost empty for the funeral service. The mourners at the graveside could be counted on one hand. Nell was given a good, respectable burial, but it was clear that the 'respectable' folk of the town had stayed away, either distancing themselves from the event or from Celia. Nicholas wondered which or why. Perhaps it was the superstition or fear related to Nell's death. She had died with her name written down in the records as Trent — an alias no doubt, not even acknowledged in death by her blood father. Nicholas grimaced at that. Why should she not have been? She was just as much a Pendleton as any other who had a blood right to claim the name.

He watched the woman, Celia, leave the graveyard with a straight back and a steady step. The vicar walked with her to the gate, his words meant to comfort her. She climbed onto the small wagon and, following on behind, Granger stepped up and took his driver's seat. A minute later he had set the vehicle moving, making off with her by his side. Her veil hid her eyes, but Nicholas suspected they were not tearful. More than anything, they were no doubt anxious to be away and free of this place, her mind no doubt set on the life in front of her in Harrogate, with all its fashion and finery. How long, he wondered, would this mother wear mourning? He had seen her longing to be in the city and craving to live a higher life in the public domain, not secreted away from the world as a hermit.

Nicholas looked around as he had done throughout the service, but had not seen or sensed any unduly watchful eyes. It appeared that the townsfolk would prefer to be done with this bad business.

'Good of you to stay for the funeral, after what happened to thee in the lock-up.' The voice spoke to him from just behind his shoulder. Nicholas glanced to his left and saw Silas Mann appear within his vision.

'The least I could do. They have not

caught him yet. It is a bad business.' Nicholas looked down the main street, past the bridge which marked the intersection of routes from north to south and east to west. The raised walkway was lined with new grand houses, which overlooked the river behind the cottages opposite. There were uniformed soldiers present now, militia at either end. Six had appeared within the town and others were on the outskirts, stopping travellers and watching for signs of the escaped felon.

'No, by God, they have not. My girls are fearful.' Silas balled his fists. He sounded angry. 'No lass is safe around here and there aren't that many young lasses in the town to spare.' He shook his head. 'What are men to do without women, eh?'

'What was the latest victim like? Was she an innocent, like this young lass Nell was?' Nicholas was surprised when the man guffawed, and then excused himself as they were still in the graveyard grounds. He gestured they should move outside.

Nicholas followed him and stopped

where the man rested against the wall on the street outside. 'You were saying?' Nicholas commented as he stood looking at Silas. Being of a height, it was easy for him to stare into the man's grey eyes. They were dulled by years of drink, but still they had a little sparkle left as he began to speak.

'Where did you get the impression Nell was 'an innocent'?' he chuckled.

Nicholas did not answer his question, but encouraged him to continue. 'She wasn't?'

Silas grinned. 'There is 'innocent' and there is 'innocent'. She was no stranger to men, but she made sure she was not caught out with a babe, if you know what I mean. She would play and tease, kiss and touch with ease. That is why she would pop in for a chat at the inn. Hoping to catch a bit of 'entertainment' and earn a few coins for her purse.' He winked.

'Did she mix with anyone in particular?' Nicholas asked.

'She weren't too particular. Neither was Sarah-Beth, but you could say that

Nell sometimes played nearer to home.' He smirked. 'Good day. I have a business to run.' He took a step away.

Nicholas grabbed his arm. The man stopped instantly and glared at Nicholas's hand. 'Remove it, or feel my fist in your face!'

Nicholas did what he was asked. 'Did Nell 'play' with the landsman Granger?'

'Aye, he liked his Nell right enough and couldn't resist playing a little.' A broad smile cut across his face and he winked. 'So what do you like, eh, stranger? What interest have you got in Guy? What have you done with him, eh?'

Nicholas's move was so quick Mann did not see it coming. Nicholas's fist landed heavily below his belly and Silas doubled up. Nicholas punched him back against the wall and pinned him there as if he were propped against it. The knife pressed to his gut kept the innkeeper from fighting back.

'Now, you listen to my words! You spread what foul rumours you care to about the dead and be damned for it, but if you say one more noise inferring such about me again then you will join them; but I can assure you that no one will find enough of the pieces of your body to give you a good send-off. You understand me?' Nicholas pressed the point of the knife to the man's gut.

'Aye, I got you.' The grey eyes looked up as he regained his breath. They looked beyond Nicholas and down the main street. 'So how will you explain this to yonder soldiers who seems to be more than a little suspicious of us? They are looking out for violent strangers, you know!'

Nicholas glanced back and could see a uniformed man watching from the far side of the bridge. He stepped back and patted Mann's shoulder with what should appear to be a friendly slap. 'No worries, friend. But remember my advice.'

Silas nodded and walked boldly away.

Nicholas gritted his teeth. If what the man implied was true, then Wilson had put the care of Celia in the hands of a man who at least he could not trust, and at worst could be their number-one suspect. How to explain this to Wilson, without having his face rearranged for besmirching the good name of his dear 'Eleanor'?

He made his way to the stables, walked beyond the stall where a hunter was stabled, and fetched out his own mount. Within moments he was riding at a pace toward the farm, still debating over which approach he would take.

9

Wilson paced up and down the hallway between the rooms. It was a sparse space with its stone floor, worn down over centuries of being trodden on. He had climbed down from the loft after the last of the soldiers had left. They had arrived as an escort for Celia, and of course his Nell — too late for that, he thought. Emotions ran out of control, wildly steaming around his mind, like the hounds of hell let loose within his brain, and they were driving him to distraction. He hated them. Emotions were a waste of energy. Love was futile; it always brought hurt along to crush your joy. He had no space in his life for either. He decided many moons since that the only satisfaction worth having was that of gratification — his own — but even this was caving in on him. He could no longer think straight. The hounds had seeped into his soul, what was left of it, when he had carelessly let his guard down. Nell had unlocked the second door, Amelia the third. Now they felt wide-open and he would not tolerate them. He would feed the hounds on the living body of the murderer who dogged his tracks and threatened his carefully balanced world. Then he would start again somewhere where he was unknown. He might even take Amelia with him — or perhaps not. He would see. First, to catch a bigger bastard than he. Wilson smiled. Set one to catch one, an old piece of wisdom he had taught Nick long since. The first door opened was still wide, yet the fool who unlatched it could not see it. He would leave it ajar and hope one day that it would be closed peaceably. The others would be sealed beyond the ability of any woman to unpick.

Some of the militia had stayed back and searched the farm grounds after her body had been taken away. Wilson had watched from a crack in the roof space. They were an unkempt bunch of ill-trained rabble. He would have whipped them into shape, literally, if he had been their commanding officer, but that was not of his concern.

Wilson returned to his present problems. Slightly calmer, he prepared his pistol, while all the time the vision of his Nell being taken away from him in a wooden box gnawed at his gut. He could not stand at her side as she was laid to rest. He never acknowledged her in life as his own blood, but in death she would be avenged as such. Then he turned his attention back to his rifle before stashing two thin blades into the top of his boots. He had discarded his long coat and chose instead his military green Rifles jacket with its striking black braid, facings and silver buttons. He was going to hide by being blatantly visible. Riding alongside Nicholas, he reasoned, they would be able to come and go at will. He was about to regain his rank and status and throw off his commoner attire. He was a man whose life had been kept orderly within his different homes and favourite clubs. He had a versatile wardrobe in each and money left at various places so that he could pick up his life in whatever port he decided to stop. It kept him on his toes, and gave him interest when he was not needed to fight another man's war. It was a life which had suited him fine, until this shadow demon had dogged his path and stolen his joy. Colonel Wilson James Pendleton was about to become visible again.

His blood boiled with rage and frustration. Eager to be about his business, he had the scent and wanted to hunt his prey. He breathed deeply, staring up at the top of the door, trying to regain his composure. He needed to see clearly, hold a steady arm and think tactically without distraction. The image of his old major crossed his thoughts and his calm was rocked again. Major Archibald Bertram Melton-Briggs now had his Amelia under his own roof. On whose damned authority? Not his, her acknowledged father's! He was her legitimate father; he had never shirked his duty as such, or as the husband of that woman — the one woman who had rejected him, the one he would have kept. Why? He asked the questions in his mind and answered his own thoughts, all the time knowing how poor a father he had been to his offspring — the ones he knew about, that was — and remiss as a husband.

He knew Major Melton-Briggs of old, from when he served as his Colonel. Wilson had had an unfortunate incident of 'mistaken' identity in the heat of battle which had fortunately removed the curse of a debt owed from an ill-placed wager, but the 'mistake' had cost Wilson his promotion and had landed him under the orders of the ex-Oxbridge associate, who had made it known he suspected him of 'foul play upon the field'. The man had not forgotten how Wilson's popularity had afforded him the upper hand in many a prank at Melton-Briggs's expense during their university days. The more Wilson pondered this fact, the more he convinced himself that the man was making a play for Amelia, and settling, no doubt, an old debt in his own cowardly way. It would not do. He would not have his daughter left in what could be seen as a compromising position with a man with a fat girth who was nearly as old as her own father. No man would ever be good enough for her in his eyes, but definitely not Melton-Briggs.

'Where the hell is Nick?' he shouted out loud as he swung his fine-weave greatcoat over his uniform and slipped his arms into the sleeves.

Ellie jumped as she had been crossing the hall as silently as she could after retrieving his tray. Her face was already flushed from crying. 'I don't know, sir.' She dipped a quick, anxious curtsey. The cutlery rattled against the pewter plate.

'Why have you been blubbering, girl?' He snapped the words at her.

'I . . . I . . . I can't help it, sir. I . . . '

'Spit it out, woman! If it's to do with that thieving vermin whom Nicholas brought here, I'll whip the lad round the stable block.'

'No . . . no, not at all! It's just that I missed the young miss's funeral and I already miss her so much. She was always singing or doing something, and the house is so quiet now, and — '

Before she could complete her sentence,

113

Wilson stood up square in front of her. Ellie froze still, realising the stupidity of uttering the truth behind her feelings to this man. 'You missed it, did you? Did I hear you complain that you missed my own daughter's funeral? Did it slip your mind that I did also? Who do you think is of more import here?' His words were shouted into her face.

Ellie did not respond to his question or rebuke. Instead she ducked back down the servants' corridor and returned to the kitchens.

He smiled momentarily; an evil glint of humour crossed his face at the show of Ellie's fear. 'Foolish wench!' he added. Once he was done here, she could close the place up and then clear out; she could always find work back in the laundry where he had found her. She deserved no better. Why had she not seen the girl slip out? The wench could have roused the mother and between them they could have stopped her. She should have looked after his Nell better. It should have been her in the box, he reasoned coolly. The boy he dismissed; he would survive on the streets, as his kind did, as vermin to gutters.

★ ★ ★

Nicholas had traversed the edge of the forest and watched the wagon on which Granger had taken Celia off toward Harrogate. He was tempted to go and thrash the truth out of the man there and then, but reasoned that, with the patrols working the area and with the clear instructions of Wilson ringing in his ears, Granger would not risk doing anything stupid on the journey. Besides, his mark was young and seemingly innocent girls; and Celia, although still attractive, was not either.

When Nicholas entered the Hall farm, Wilson was waiting for him, giving the impression he had been sitting there for some time, silently poised upon the bottom step, with his rifle pointed straight at Nicholas's chest. 'You kept me waiting, Nick!' He tilted his face upwards; deeply troubled eyes stared at Nicholas.

'I was unexpectedly delayed.' Nicholas

115

looked back at him. He could not help but note that there was a strange stillness to his manner, the calm before a proverbial storm. 'We have a lead, sir.' Nicholas watched for his reaction, unsure how it would come; but come it would — and no doubt suddenly or violently. The presence of the uniform told Nicholas he was now ready to kill.

Wilson stood up and strode toward him holding the rifle in his hand, whilst carrying a small pack in the other. 'Speak, man!' He dropped the pack at Nicholas's feet. 'Have you lost your wits? Tell me what 'lead' it is that you think we have.'

Nicholas had rarely seen Wilson so ruffled. Even in the cell he was calm; but now his need to vent his anger, to rip the murderer apart, was apparent to Nicholas, as he knew how to read this man's character. He had seen that wild, almost mad glint in Wilson's eyes before a battle. If he were a wild dog, he would be ready to attack his prey, coiled like a spring, teeth ready to rip out the throat of his victim. Nick wondered how the hell he was going to explain the news about

Granger to him when he was in this state, without risking him shooting anyone who stood in his way — including himself, possibly.

'Mount up, sir.' Nicholas picked up his senior's pack. 'I'll explain on the way there.' Nicholas went to turn away, but Wilson was having none of it.

'Stand and talk, man!' he ordered.

Nicholas could see the nervous face of Guy hiding in the shadows of the servants' corridor. The lad seemingly never missed a trick. Nicholas did not want him to become involved in the exchange which would trigger the next part of their plight. Nicholas needed to be able to control what was about to unfold. One mad fist striking out from Wilson could kill the boy. Nicholas was only too aware of what the man's fist felt like; but in this cold rage, one blow could be deadly.

'Sir, we need to speak with Granger. He may hold the clue to this . . . affair.' Nicholas saw the bemusement cross Wilson's face. He tried to catch Guy's eye, to gesture to him to get clear, but the boy either could not pick up the hidden message or was too curious to save him the possibility of more trouble.

'Don't you think that if he held any information which would help, he would have spoken it out? He has been watching over my women for nearly ten years. The man owes me dearly. He would not challenge my authority or trust, for I can have him arrested and thrown into the debtors' gaol in a trice. You know what that is like, don't you, Nick, my boy?' He paused.

Nicholas ignored the jibe. He was not going to rise to such an obvious goading.

'Why? What would possess you to say such a thing?' Wilson's stare was intense, slicing across the emotions; he was suppressing his anxiety to be on the chase, to focus on Nicholas's words.

'What do you know of their lives here over those ten years, sir? Where were you for most of this time?' Nicholas saw Wilson raise his eyebrow, taken aback by the possible rebuke.

'You know where I have been, for you have served with me for most of it. I have returned whenever I could visit my 'dear wife'.' The corner of his mouth almost developed a form of tic, as if he wanted to smile at the irony of his words, but his state of mind would not let him. This was indeed a warning to Nicholas. He was almost beyond his own control. Nicholas knew then what he had to do; but as his instructor had taught him, he gave nothing of his intentions away.

'He may be the murderer. He knew your movements — when you were returning, and how. He knew your plans. He had reason, perhaps, to break free of your grip. In other words, he had sufficient reason to hate you and frame you dead to rights.' Nicholas saw Wilson take in each statement and add it to the previous one. He had no wish to besmirch a dead girl's reputation further by stating what the innkeeper had told him. If he could make a convincing enough case from what he already knew and from what Wilson had just told him, then he could omit that girl's behaviour from his story.

'Come!' Wilson stormed past Nicholas,

which was the moment the latter struck out. Wilson fell to the ground, floored by a swift blow to the temple. Guy ran out from the cover of the shadows as he witnessed Nicholas's unprovoked blow.

'You done it now, mister!' he said, as he ran to Wilson's collapsed form. 'He's out cold! You two have the strangest friendship I ever seen.'

'Get Ellie, whilst I move him. We need a secure room where he can be locked in and left undisturbed. I doubt the militia will return, but I need to keep him here for his own safety, whilst I sort out Granger.' Nicholas had been surprised by the lad's comments. Why on earth had he presumed they were friends? Guy ran off, to return with a very flustered Ellie tagging behind.

'Lord help us!' she cried as she saw Wilson's body draped over Nicholas's shoulder. 'He'll kill you, for sure!'

'Never mind that. Lead me to the store rooms and bring a strong rope.'

10

Nicholas was led to an empty store room, which had no window within it, as the cellar had been dismissed because it had other entrances. He dragged a chair inside this erstwhile cell and bound Wilson to it, then told Ellie to wrap a poultice on the bump which was starting to show on the man's head. He had removed the pistol and retrieved the blades from the man's boots. Nicholas suppressed an urge to smile as he too had had his boots adapted to take similar weapons. They added an element of surprise when cornered in a back alley. He had learned many a sound and a harsh lesson from his officer. Once this was done, he sent Ellie outside.

'What the hell do you think you are doing?' a bleary voice murmured, still very dazed.

Nicholas propped the man's head up, cupped within his hands. The lids half opened but were fighting a losing battle. 'Forgive me, Father, for I have sinned . . . ' Nicholas said, as he patted the man's shoulder, 'but, in doing so, I am, I believe, saving your life. We will have the man arrested and let the law do their worst. You will not bloody your hands here; this is England, and not a battleground in some foreign land.'

The head slumped. Nicholas walked away, locking the door behind him. He left him there and needed to reach Granger before they arrived in Harrogate.

Guy followed him to the stables. 'Let me come with you? I can be your ears and watch your back.'

'You would have to be very versatile and busy to do both. No, Guy; I need someone here to stay with Ellie. I am not sure if she is strong enough to resist Wilson's pleas if he begs her for help.' Nicholas looked at him earnestly.

Guy looked as if he were not convinced that this argument was credible.

'Do you think I would be stupid enough to open the door to that madman?' Ellie said from the doorway. 'Take him with you. If anything goes wrong with your plans you will need to get word back to me. He can be your mouthpiece as well as your ears. Take this, too.' She held out a bundle of ham, cheese and bread.

Nicholas was conscious of the amount of time slipping through his fingers. 'Very well, but you obey me to the letter. If I say run, Guy, you run!'

'Yes, sir!' The boy jumped to attention and tried to salute.

'Very good. Remember it well.' Nicholas mounted the horse and pulled Guy onto the saddle in front of him. He walked the animal past Ellie.

'Ellie, under no circumstances open the door or go inside that room to Wilson. He may promise you the world, but do not trust him.' He looked at her, weighting his words with as much warning as he could muster.

'You think you need to tell me that, Mister Penn?'

'I suppose not, but I am warning you to take care.'

'How did you find out about Granger?' Ellie asked.

'You knew they were more than a little 'friendly' with each other?' Nicholas glanced down at the woman's face, which was amazingly relaxed. 'You didn't try to warn her?'

'Oh, aye, like she'd listen to me, I don't think! Sure I told her that, but he'd have skinned the pair of them if he'd known, so we kept it hushed up. And when we heard he was coming back, things reverted to how he expected them to be. But I hadn't got him down for a murderer.' Ellie hugged herself and shivered. 'Ain't nowhere safe these days. Can't trust no one, can thee. I'll not let the colonel out, on that you can be sure. But me bag will be packed and I'll thank you for a lift to town when all this is done. I want to be out of here long before he is.' She nodded toward the Hall farm. 'I'll have to trust in you, I guess.'

'You can, and I promise you will be.'

Nicholas made good speed as they crossed the countryside and cut a chunk off their journeying time. Light would be closing in soon. Just as well they had been given some food. It had been the furthest thing from his mind. Once within reach of his target, he paused within the cover of some trees ahead of the wagon along the road. There he left Guy, watching and helping himself to the food, whilst he galloped over to the wagon as it made its last turn of the road, before passing the trees on the road into Harrogate.

'What news?' Granger asked, obviously thrown by Nicholas's presence on the road in front of them. He stopped the wagon, seeing Nicholas approach.

Nicholas rode alongside him, facing Granger. He noted the anxiety showing on Celia's face at his sudden appearance. Her eyes were scouting the woods as if she expected Wilson to appear as a spectre, come to haunt her. Love was not an aspect which Nicholas could see as any part of their 'arrangement'.

'We need to talk. Step down here. I have word from Colonel Pendleton. Pull the wagon over there. It won't take a minute, ma'am.' He offered her what he had hoped was a reassurance.

Granger nodded and moved the wagon to the side, securing its brake. Nicholas dismounted and tied the horse to the wagon. He knew Granger was wary and watching for him to make any movement which would give away any intention other than to talk to him in confidence.

Nicholas kept his manner even, trying not to give away that he knew that Granger was a callous murderer. Nicholas would not underestimate him. They strode to the edge of the woods ahead of the wagon.

'Be quick!' Celia shouted.

Granger looked at Nicholas with a hint of reaction. He was no fool; Nicholas knew he had the sense to feel when something was up. 'So, what does the colonel want to tell us?'

Nicholas nodded. 'No, not the colonel, but you. I want you to tell me what the relationship was you had with young Nell. Be honest, or I will inform Pendleton that you and she were . . . ' Nicholas was poised with his hand on a knife under the cover of his coat. He would have him if he went for his pistol. However, to his surprise he did not respond with an attack. Instead a bemused face stared at him.

'You are so wrong, man. I thought of the lass like me own daughter. But she would only look up to her real pa for authority when he was there. I never done anything to the lass which wasn't proper. She was a wild child. She took her blood from him.' He stared back blankly.

Nicholas was completely thrown by his resignation to the accusation. Ellie had also said that they had been carrying on, hadn't she? So, what had she meant? Unless . . . He glanced back at Celia. She had inched forward on the seat and had heard the accusation.

'He would never have touched the girl. But she was too flighty for her own good. She liked to tease the pair of us. She thought our lives were those of fools. She bribed us.' Celia climbed down and ran the few steps to take her place next to Granger, who protectively placed an arm around her shoulders. Her defiant eyes explained all.

'You two are lovers?' Nicholas asked, knowing the answer. 'He would indeed skin you both alive before he saw reason for this betrayal. Good grief, man! How

many years have you been together?'
Nicholas saw the commitment between
them and also that one element which
had been missing from Celia and Wilson's
union — love.

'Nearly ten,' Celia admitted.

Granger stepped protectively forward, placing himself between Celia and
Nicholas. 'For her sake, man, don't tell
the colonel. She's entitled to a life as well.
He had her holed up there so as he could
visit his wife and child, but then make
merry with this poor wench and spoil
Eleanor so that she had no manners
worth a lady having. He let her do
whatever she wished when he was there:
ride, hunt, wander. Is it any wonder that
she started venturing further afield when
she was so bored and was waiting for his
next visit? We fell in love. We were lonely,
and well . . . '

'You didn't think that Mr Granger
could have been the murderer, did you?'
Celia asked.

Granger's head shot around. 'Don't
be a bloody fool, man. I had what I
wanted here: the farm, my woman and a

headstrong but adorable daughter of sorts. Why would I destroy that, to go back to the city and be locked away for gambling debts? No, man, I had it all. Who the hell put that thought in your head?' He shook his head in disbelief.

'Never mind that. Go to your new home, and take care not to be found out. I have a very angry colonel to deal with as it is; you really do not want to have him take his wrath out on the two of you.' Nicholas remounted, realising this was a wild goose chase and that Mann had put two and two together and made five. Stupidly, Nicholas realised that he had fed Granger's name to the man whose blood would be beyond the boil. If Wilson escaped now . . . Hell! What a mess he was making of this.

'You won't split on us?' Granger asked. 'You know what he'd do.'

Nicholas looked at Celia. 'I will try to set things right, but keep a good watch out. The colonel is grieving, angry and wild. He wants to find this man who has shattered his world and threatened his liberty. No, I will not tell on you two, but he may well suspect you.'

'Then I will put him straight on that. Thank you.' Granger saluted Nicholas.

'Don't thank me. It's on your conscience, not mine.'

Celia laughed openly. 'You think Wilson knows what a conscience is?'

'God speed. Take care to bolt all doors till this business is sorted,' Nicholas said, as he did not want to answer the question. What they did was literally their own affair. Right now he had a bigger problem. If Granger was not the murderer, then he had better find out bloody quick who was, because Wilson would not stay incarcerated for long. He would have to be released, and Nicholas needed to present the guilty party before him to protect the innocent who would get in Wilson's way once the man took to his own search. He retrieved Guy from his vantage point and made straight for the old manor house, the scene of the last murder. Perhaps there he would find a clue as to where to go next.

11

The manor was a place which Nicholas knew well from his childhood. He had travelled in silence as he rode at the gallop, making his way to one of the Pendleton family estates. This most northern one had been the country home of Elizabeth Mary Pendleton and Amelia Louise Pendleton, who had been brought up a lady and was about to come out this season in London. He knew all of this and the excitement the girl had about the prospect of being exposed to the 'marriage market'. Her anxiety that her pianoforte playing should be found wanting, or that her manners or bearing might be considered to be too common, had been increasing. Her gowns would be the finest fashion Harrogate could offer and the quality was second to none, but beneath the finery she felt that her northern upbringing and her private tutors might well have left her wanting.

All this Amelia had revealed to Nicholas in her infrequent letters. He had of course tried to reassure her that her father would never allow her to be in a position where she could be shamed by being ill-prepared. The man had settled an attractive sum upon her at the mother's insistence, but Nicholas also knew that any cad who tried to grasp it and woo Amelia would be dealt with sharply by Wilson. This was something Amelia would never have understood, as her naivety was her most appealing quality — which also left her vulnerable in a world of jackals.

Nicholas also felt protective of her, but his priority was to see that the father did not crush all chance the daughter had of attaining a happy marriage. Now Nell had been taken from him, the grip upon Amelia's future, Nicholas feared, would be even tighter — as suffocating as her mother's had been.

Nicholas stopped outside the gamekeeper's cottage. He placed a breathless Guy on the ground, his legs a little unsteady after experiencing his first long ride at a gallop. The light had almost gone, giving way to a moonlit sky. It would be a cold night as there was no cloud cover.

Nicholas rapped on the door with his fist. It was flung open wide and lamplight was shone directly in his face. He sensed a pistol was being pointed at him in the man's other hand. A wise precaution, Nicholas thought. He felt Guy move behind him.

'James, it is me, Nicholas.'

'Goodness, man, now I do believe in miracles. I never thought to see you here again. You nearly had your head blowed clean off. The wife is so scared of the Monster of Gorebeck, that anyone who comes near is in her sights before I can grab the gun myself.' He lowered the lamp and Nicholas saw the man's familiar face. It was some years older, the lines a little deeper and the eyes not as bright as they had once been when he, Nicholas, had been forced to leave the place, but the man seemed to be the same character in essence. James glanced down at Guy. 'He yours?' He flashed the lamp at the boy.

'Not by blood; but by circumstance, he is with me. Can we come in? I need to talk to you about what happened here. Time is of the essence, James.'

The man stepped back into his simple cottage and made way for Nicholas and Guy to enter. The inside had only two proper chairs and a small stool. The cottage had two rooms and he had a wife and four children. The place was warmed by a fire, where a stew pot hung and a kettle was kept warm on the hearth. For all it lacked in material finery, the smiles on the faces of these people made Nicholas feel as though he had been welcomed into a much-loved home. He could see the same thoughts in Guy's expression as he sheepishly looked at a young girl of about the lad's age. The other children were younger.

'It's a bad business, Mr Nicholas. If that bas — ' He glanced at his wife. 'If the murderer is not found soon, people will be accusing their neighbours of it. We'll end up with witch hunts again. You know what I mean. Better to hang someone for a crime than accept that none's been caught.' He gestured for Nicholas to take the chair.

'Yes I do know, exactly.' Nicholas shook his head. He did not want to stop here; he needed to push on. 'Which is why I need to dig him out before more innocence can be crushed by his hands. I need to know what happened here, and see where it happened. The colonel also wants blood for this outrage.' Nicholas saw James and his wife exchange worried looks at the mention of Wilson's name.

'Is he coming here . . . tonight? The house is all locked up. Major Melton-Briggs gave orders for it to be. We had to do as he said, he being the magistrate, you know, and . . . ' He cleared his throat. 'Colonel Pendleton's rarely here, isn't he?'

Nicholas ignored the rebuke, but acknowledged that the man was in his rights to make it. 'Can we go? You can tell me what happened as we look around. Then I will need to sleep a few hours, so a bed would be welcome, but I will be gone before dawn. Colonel Pendleton is not with me; he is rather tied up at the moment and has been delayed.' Nicholas saw Guy grin, but he shot him a warning look and the lad returned to his normal deadpan expression. His eyes sparkled as he took in everything around him, accepting a piece of tea bread from the young girl.

James slipped his jacket on, picked up his pistol and lamp and let them back out into the night air.

'Do you want to stay here?' Nicholas asked Guy.

'No, sir, I is coming with you,' he answered, and slipped past both men and out into the open air.

James shut the cottage door, ordering his wife to bar it from the inside.

'So what happened here, and when?' Nicholas asked as James walked them in the direction of the barn.

'It were early Monday morning. She had done the wash and had hung it up. She must have seen something over in the barn and gone in to look. There were no tracks of her being dragged in. I'd have seen them a mile off if that were the case. Then he . . . well, he must have got the drop on her and pinned her down. Looks like she had little chance or time to struggle. She was found half naked and with blood seeping out of her side. How he had not been seen by someone, I don't know. He left his hat, but he must have had blood on him. Anyways, he must have knocked her out, as she was just laid there. No one heard nothing. It was like he was a phantom who came, killed and went. A demon . . . '

'Talk like that will set people's minds afire, James. Quell it. This is a man, not a beast or a spirit.' They reached the entrance to the barn. James picked up a lamp, which he left on the side hook of the door, and lit it for Nicholas.

'Where?' he asked. He followed the direction in which James's finger pointed. There was a place where the hay was discoloured and disturbed. Guy had followed in and seen Nicholas's hat thrown to the side.

Nicholas walked carefully and sequentially back and forth from the door to the place where she was murdered. The soldiers had disturbed much of the hay, but he could still see the place where she had been laid quite clearly.

'See, there is no sign of dragging or a fight,' James said proudly, knowing he was right about that.

Nicholas was deep in thought.

'She must have seen something which caught her eye and, instead of coming for me or for my Gemma, she went looking herself.' James scratched his grizzled chin. 'I don't come in here much. I should have swept the place out, but don't think it's right to do that just yet. I'm not a soft man, but this business . . . well, it has given me the creeps. If I got my hands on him, I would string him up by the . . . you see if I don't.'

'There is another possibility.' Nicholas looked across at him after examining the place closely where the girl had fallen. 'An obvious one, yet seemingly missed by all.'

'She knew him already. Didn't she, Mr Penn?' Guy asked, confidently.

Nicholas grinned at the lad, admiring his intelligence. 'Yes, lad. I think she knew him. Not only are there no marks of her being dragged, but all the marks hereabouts show the minimum of struggle. This is not the scene of a murder where a woman was taken by surprise and fought for her life.' His eyes caught sight of a glint amongst the soiled strewn hay as he moved the light. Ignoring the blood-stained hay half covering it, he picked it up and wiped it against the fresh straw to remove the dried blood, revealing the gilt edge of a button. The centre was bone. This roughly made button might be nothing, but it was all Nicholas had found that was a possible physical clue.

'Is this yours?' he asked James. Guy strained to see it, but said nothing.

'Nope, and it certainly isn't off the militia's uniforms.' James looked to the door. The night sky was setting in; they could see their own breath as they spoke, the air was so cold.

'Take us to the house and we will sleep there for a few hours,' Nicholas instructed.

'Aye. Give my regards to the colonel when you meet up with him. I suppose we'll be seeing him soon enough.' James's remark held little enthusiasm.

Nicholas nodded and prepared himself to set foot in the manor house — a place he had sworn he would never enter again as long as he lived. But tonight he was glad to be drawing breath and living. He was tired, and as he placed a hand upon Guy's shoulders, as if giving him support, he realised to his surprise that he was grateful not to be on his own too.

12

Five hours' sleep had given Nicholas a fresh and clear head with which to think. Granger was an unlikely candidate, although marginally still possible. The magistrate, the major, would hardly get his hands dirty and risk all the reputation he had built up in the world for the sake of an Oxbridge grudge. Revenge had been given him when Wilson was refused his majority, his excellent reputation as a daring soldier upon the field tarnished for life. He stared out of the long windows above the central stairwell and scanned the ground before him. Who else? There was the innkeeper who had cast the doubt over Granger, yet his observations and misconception were understandable. He knew Nell — he said himself he had spoken to her — but did he know Sarah-Beth? He had an establishment to run, so how would he be free to roam and prey, and how would he have known where Wilson was? He was known to the townsfolk as James Wilson, a civilian — not in his role as Colonel Pendleton, elusive absent figure from the manor house. No, Silas had not the knowledge needed to have completed the murders, even if he had the means he lacked the motive and, Nicholas suspected, the intelligence. So who did that leave? Wilson? In his heart he could not bear to believe he would, even if he knew the man could. He had a soul which he could somehow detach from himself from when 'duty' demanded it. He glanced over to the barn. Who had Sarah-Beth seen? Who did she trust to be that close to her in a confined space? It had to be someone she knew.

The sun was yet to announce a new day, but he was washed, dressed and ready to go, having eaten the food Gemma had left for him in the dining room. He could not resist a quick tour of the place; but then, as he saw a painting of Elizabeth Pendleton glaring accusingly at him, he decided it was time to go and face his past. Strange — he had stood before a French column and stayed calm, yet the woman's eyes, even in a painting, made his gut knot with gnarled memories; and so he made his way down the stairs to ready his horse. He had let the lad sleep on, debating whether he should wake him or not, take him with him or leave him behind for his own safety, when the voice took him completely by surprise.

'Thought you'd be heading here once your wild chase had turned up a complete goose.' Wilson's words resounded down the length of the stables as he stepped out of the end stall. In his greatcoat and officer's hat he looked impressive, even to Nicholas, even though he had seen him so attired on many an occasion. He held a crop in his hand; it was idly hanging at his side, being flicked slowly back and forth. The poultice must have worked, for Nicholas could just see only a slight bruise below his hat's rim. If anything, he was perhaps showing his seniority in years slightly more than he had three months earlier, when they had parted on the steps of a coffee house in St James near

Piccadilly, London.

'What did you do with Ellie, sir?' Nicholas was damned annoyed with himself, knowing he had left the woman unprotected with this man in an empty house, miles from the nearest help. He should have guessed that Wilson would find a way out.

'She has left us for a more challenging future. She took the money which I offered her and, I would add, paid her more than fairly; and with my promise that I would not seek my revenge upon her, she decided to go on her way. Ellie has started upon her journey to visit her sister in Newcastle, I believe. So at least one person is happy with their lot in this miserable affair. And who knows, maybe more than she will be celebrating their good fortune today.' He approached Nicholas. 'Not least the vermin who thinks he can dog my tracks and take from me those whom I have chosen to hold dear.'

'Do you intend to try and thrash me with that?' Nicholas asked as he pointed to the crop. 'Or are you now calm enough for us to work together? Granger is not the man we seek, of that I am sure. His actions were ... misunderstood.' Nicholas took in Wilson's every gesture. The storm appeared to have abated and his persona was more rational — not a twitch discernible; no jittery behaviour. A more normal — for Wilson at least — detached calm ensued.

'No. We are wasting precious time fighting amongst ourselves; we need to sort this out, I agree. Granger is not the man, granted; I could have told you that, once my rage had passed me by. I have had time to think. He could not have been there when I was in Whitby, for he would have still been tucked up in Celia's bed.' Wilson laughed as Nicholas's face showed his shock at the evenness of the revelation within Wilson's words.

'Dear boy, do you not think I am aware of the situation there? She has been a good woman to me and he a loyal servant; they suit each other well and in truth I tire of them both. They now lose the farm; they have three months' rent paid on the house in Harrogate. She shall

145

find suitable clothes waiting for her and he will be handed a letter of introduction to a landowner who is in need of a reliable man — an overseer. So they will be well set up and served a further instruction from my representative who will explain that from the day the lease expires, they will have to fund their own lifestyle. His debtor's notes will be returned to him and he will no longer be in my pocket. However, they will have to fend for themselves. I am setting them both free.' Wilson leaned against a stall, watching Nicholas's puzzled expression, and openly grinned at him.

'Why are you being so generous? Have you suddenly seen the light? You let Ellie leave unharmed, paid off, and you expect me to believe that you are setting these two, who have betrayed your trust, free also? Why do I find this hard to accept, sir? Just as you hold a crop in your hand, yet you have not attempted a rebuke or to indulge in an act of vengeance against my person for my tying you up and leaving you under lock and key. What game is it you play now, sir? What test or trap are you setting for us?' Nicholas faced him.

'You see through me, partially. Ellie will arrive in Newcastle to discover her sister has passed away two years since. She has no home to go to and will have to make her own way in life. I wish her well. She has two strong arms and if she chooses not to use them she can always lay on her back, she is young enough,' he said dryly. 'Granger is a gambler. He has not imbibed of much since he arrived at the farm because he only plays dice once a week in the inn in the local town, and Silas Mann is instructed not to allow him to lose more than a few pennies; but he keeps his hand in with the gaming and his thirst is as great now as it was ten years ago. Harrogate has many opportunities for a gambler to sip from the cup of destruction and he will initially have a few pounds in his purse to decide what he should do with his newly found freedom. So, will love and responsibility conquer his thirst, or will he still end up in the debtors' gaol, once more? His fate is in his own hands.' Wilson shrugged his shoulders dismissively.

'What about Celia? Do you care not for her? She is the mother of one of your children.' Nicholas saw Wilson scoff at the word 'care'.

'My dear boy, you have the heart of a romantic and not a soldier after all. If she had cared for my Nell, then she would still be grieving deeply now. She would no more go from her daughter's funeral to the arms of her lover in the same day. She will discover for herself what fate she has chosen over security in a few months' time. The answer to that puzzle will be revealed by the fates, but I will not look on; for sincerely, my dear boy, I care not anymore. My interest in her was murdered with Nell. Spare me the disappointed look. You are not new to the idea that I have sired bastards, man, but at least I provided for the ones who knew me at all.' Wilson's ebony eyes stared into Nicholas's. 'As for you, Nick. You did well. You caught me unprepared, off guard and at a disadvantage. True, you wasted more time — as we do now — but you acted like a soldier. You took decisive action when your superior was momentarily lost to anger and

148

grief. What is more to the point, I did not see it coming. You got the drop on me first time, Nick. I actually feel proud that you proved that you have listened to me over the years.' He clapped Nicholas on his shoulder. 'Well done!'

'Thank you, sir,' Nicholas replied, but he was indeed wary. If he had bested his superior, would Wilson now look on him as a threat?

'However, you ever pull a trick like that on me again and I will make sure you never raise a hand to me or anyone in the duration of your lifetime again!' He slapped Nicholas's shoulder a couple more times and then pointed to his horse. 'You had best mount up. We are going to visit my family. It is time 'Papa' reclaimed his womenfolk. Do you have any leads, man? Because if not, I strongly suspect the answer to this riddle lies behind the person or will of a magistrate, so we have our work cut out. Come, we will talk more on the way.'

Nicholas walked his horse out of the stables. James had appeared, pulling on his jacket, and was greeting his master anxiously. Obviously he did not wish to be found wanting.

Guy ran out of the house. 'Mr Penn, wait!'

Wilson looked at Nicholas. 'Lose him; he'll be in the way.' He turned the horse around and started to walk it down the drive.

'James, look after him for me until I return,' Nicholas shouted.

'Aye, lad, I'll do that.' The gamekeeper gestured to the lad to come into his cottage.

'Mr Penn . . . ' Guy's cries faded as Nick rode away, wondering why he had promised to return for the boy. He was quickly becoming the lad's benefactor, a notion which strangely he found appealed.

Both men left. The boy fell silent. Nicholas placed his hand in his pocket and felt the broken button. Perhaps this could be the lead they needed, but Wilson had already kicked his horse on into a gallop and was streaking ahead of him as he left the manor grounds for the open track which would cross in the direction of the major's estate. Nicholas joined him. Now his colonel had regained his senses, Nicholas wondered how they would deal with a major who outranked both the colonel and him — only a captain, not even in uniform. His world was becoming more challenging; yet despite his frequent feelings of disgust at Wilson's behaviour, he could not help but admire how he was capable of seeing his 'justice' done by letting people decide their own way to ruin.

13

'Gemma, take the lad inside and give him some food, there's a love.' James looked down at him and winked. 'It's been a right old mess for sure. You're best out of it, lad.'

'How can I watch 'is back if I ain't with him to do it?' Guy complained.

'Well, perhaps men like that don't need their back watching. They've been through war and much worse watching each other's.' James smiled warmly at him, then gestured he go inside.

'That Wilson, I don't trust 'im. He is evil. He could turn on Mr Penn, and he is such a good gent!' Guy defended the only person who had helped him since he lost his family. Mann did not count, because he had worked the lad hard for his meagre rations.

'Rest assured, he'll not hurt young Nick in any way. He'd die first. Of that you can be sure. Now go on with you. I have work to do; you stay and watch my Gemma's back. There's still a murderer about.' He winked at the lad as if he was really trying to befriend his trust.

Reluctantly, Guy stayed inside the cottage. The woman left him in the care of her daughter, who welcomed him warmly, which made him feel even more uneasy. This was getting a sight too cosy for a lad who was used to being in the open air and on his own, he reasoned.

★ ★ ★

Wilson obviously had no intention of talking anything through on the ride. He seemed completely absorbed in his own thoughts. Nicholas pulled up alongside. Guiltily, he wondered if the man's head still throbbed, but knew better than to ask him.

'What do you intend to do, sir?' Nicholas asked. 'I still think that Mann is the strongest contender for both Nell's and possibly Sarah-Beth's murders. The others will need further investigation to see if he was out of town at the time, but if we can pin either of the local ones on him then that will make it easier to ascertain when or how he did the others — when they knew your tracks. He is a rough bastard and if he has a jacket which has a broken or missing button that matches this, then we have our man. But, the orders could have come from the major. If so, how we prove it will be a damned difficult task, unless he confesses it, that is. We could help him unburden himself.' Nicholas held out the broken button in his palm so that Wilson could see it.

The man did not respond, initially. Then: 'I will know when I see the major, what part — if any — he has in this.'

Nicholas replaced the fragment of button, amazed, as they continued in silence.

★   ★   ★

Inside the cottage, Guy was becoming increasingly restless; the girl's chatter was driving him to distraction.

'Where are your ma and pa?' she asked, as her mother took the basket outside to fetch more wood for the small fire. She had refused Guy's offer of help. He suspected that she, too, was eager to go out.

'Both dead,' he said simply, as they sat podding the freshly-picked peas.

'What about your brothers and sisters? Do you have any?' she persisted, keeping half her attention on the three younger children who were huddled together on the makeshift cot where they slept.

'No,' he answered, having no wish to discuss the loss of anyone else. He wanted to forget the misery and the loneliness. In the last few days he had had the company of someone who treated him right. He had seen beyond the town and he wanted to be with Mr Penn again.

'Must be very hard for you,' she continued.

'No, I get by.' He looked at the children on the bed, curled into one another for comfort and warmth. This was not for him.

'He used to live here, Pa said — your 'Mr Penn' — although he don't think you should call him that really. Best to use his name.'

Guy looked up at the rebuke, wondering

why he should have the right to call Mr Penn 'Nicholas', especially as it had already been made clear to him what he should call him. It was none of her business anyways. He flicked a row of peas out of the pod in disgust.

'The mistress threw them both out. Strange, eh?' she added. 'Do you know why?'

'No,' he replied, his eyes scanning the cottage for any type of distraction.

'I hate it when Pa goes away. You must get lonely. I do, and we are a family.' Her voice drifted across him, as he took an inventory of their poverty. Perhaps, he reasoned, the 'homeliness' of the initial impression was just misjudged — a first impression after them being out in the cold for so long.

Then he looked up at her. She smiled, grateful to have his full attention at last. She was pretty. He realised he had been looking around the cottage for something to distract him when what he was seeking was sitting in front of him. So she had her wish, because his attention was now totally hers.

Wilson walked boldly into the office of his ex-commanding officer, with Nicholas following a couple of steps behind him. His eyes scanned everything around them, realising that they were in a lavishly decorated hall which had enough staff within it to overpower them in a fight-or-flight situation.

'By Gad, sir! Pendleton, I had no idea where the hell you were. Are you acquainted with the horrendous facts of what occurred at your farm, man?' He stood up and gestured that Wilson should sit down in the chair opposite his desk.

The major was more rounded in stature than when Nicholas had seen him a year previously, when he had returned to England with the colonel, both having served their dues for King and Country. He stood to the side of the doorway, not expecting an acknowledgment of his presence.

'I was on my way home; and yes, I am. I wish to remove my daughter and wife from here and reinstate them in my Mayfair residence. I thank you for your swift actions and placing them in the safety of your own home. Have you apprehended the murderer yet?' Wilson had sat down and crossed his legs, removing his hat and placing it across his lap.

'Of course, I shall arrange for an escort to take you down country. I was not expecting that the ladies should stay here for long.'

Nicholas noted a hint of relief in the Major's face and wondered if Mrs Pendleton was proving to be a more troublesome guest than he had expected.

'We have not apprehended the man. He escaped from the lock-up. A man called Wilson, strangely enough — alias, no doubt. He had been known to stay in the town, gambling. Never more than a stopover for a few days. The man seemed to keep very much to himself. The innkeeper said he'd recognise him on sight. Blackguard disappeared without a trace, then that lass was murdered at your farm. Hell, man! Why would you leave your women alone in such a place? I don't understand you. You hardly set foot outside of London, so why not have them with you there?' The major's cheeks were flushed but the passion in his words seemed genuinely meant. 'I know you can be a bastard, Wilson, but to your own womenfolk?' He shook his head.

'You have it wrong, Major. I did not send her there. She insisted upon the move, knowing my business interests in London would keep me in the city most of the year.' Wilson watched the surprise upon the major's face.

Nicholas knew that there was some truth in his colonel's words, but he knew the full story and he hoped for Elizabeth's and Amelia's sake he would not expand upon his answer further to the major, for that would be purely cruel and serve no purpose but to damage their name.

'Very well, that is your affair. I will have them join you in the gallery; you can make your peace and arrangements there.' He hesitated. 'Pendleton, that girl of yours — she is quite a sweet thing. I don't suppose you would consider an offer of — '

'Yes!' Wilson snapped the word out, causing a moment of optimism to show in the major's eyes. 'Yes, you are quite right, sir. I would not consider an offer for her as she has yet to 'come out' in society, and I have every intention of seeing this happen.'

'As I said, Pendleton, you can be a right bastard when you wish to be even under my own roof. There are more grateful wenches out there for the plucking. I wish her well and God help the man whom you saddle her with, for he will have you as his father-in-law. A terrible thought, that — eh, Nicholas?' he spluttered out the remark as he laughed and pulled the bell cord. 'I will have you both shown to the gallery. There will be a coach made ready to transport them in two days' time, which should give the ladies time to have their clothes repacked.'

A manservant arrived. 'Show my guests to the gallery and then fetch Miss Amelia and the colonel's good lady wife. Good day, sirs,' he said, and then he returned to his desk and what he had been doing.

★　★　★

They stood side-by-side in the gallery, both contemplating the reunion which would shortly befall them, in their own ponderous way. 'Do you think he is involved?' Nicholas asked.

'No, though it confounds me to admit it. This makes this situation even more of a mess than the immediate one we face, Nick. What do we say? Keep it as sweet as possible for Amelia's sake. I know you care for her.'

Nicholas flushed slightly. 'We have kept in touch over the years, sir,' Nicholas admitted.

'I know that. How do you think that the letters and her notes find their way back and forth without the help of my trusty servants? Don't be so naïve; it does not become you.'

Nicholas looked at the man. 'I thought you would have disapproved. Did she really choose to live here? The exile from London really was not of your doing?' he asked in a lowered tone.

'Nick, I never wanted the family to be split up. Yet you cannot even bear to share a name. She made me choose, and I chose you!'

14

Guy had watched Molly intensely; the slight flush to her cheeks told him she liked him being there. This made it so much easier for Guy to get her talking, and diverting her questions to him. She sat opposite him at the hearth, perched on a small stool, relaxed as she did her mending, content with her newfound friend. Guy looked at what she was doing. Her stitches were neat, considering that there wasn't much of a selection of threads, needles, and bits and bobs in the small tin; but she was deft at handling an old needle.

'You do all the mending here?' he asked casually as he flicked the last pea from its pod and stifled a yawn. Some of them had slipped into his mouth — a sweet treat.

'Yes. Ma's eyes aren't as sharp as they used to be.' She pulled on the worn trouser fabric to ease the weight onto her small knee so that the cloth lay flat, ready for her to repair the broken fastening.

Guy stood up, stretched and casually walked toward the door.

'They didn't say that you could leave, Guy. You best wait here till Pa returns. He won't like it if you walk off. He promised Mr Nicholas that you would be here safe.' Her eyes looked hopefully at him as she obviously had enjoyed having some company — or more specifically, his.

'I need to pee, Molly,' he answered bluntly, and he put his hand on the door handle.

'Well, in that case, of course you must, but be quick. Ma will be back with the wood and she will need a bit of help. She'll be cross if you dally; there is a madman at loose,' she warned him, and then smiled reassuringly.

Guy nodded and returned the gesture warmly, for he knew she meant well, and then he slipped out of the door.

★　★　★

Nicholas studied the hung oil paintings down the panelled sides of the long gallery — ancestors of the major, no doubt. They were similar in their stature and bulldog expression, especially the women, he mused. However, Wilson's admission had both surprised and touched him; he had done the man a disservice in his judgement of him over the years. Nicholas realised he had in fact judged him harshly, almost as much as Elizabeth had done. This was neither the time nor place to take that particular conversation further; but once again, his colonel had wrong-footed him. His eyes followed the Elizabethan gallery along and up to the minstrel's balcony above. Wilson stood next to him.

'He chose wisely. The acoustics in here travel well. Designed for it, I would say.'

Nicholas nodded slightly; he had realised the same thing. These walls had ears.

The doors at the opposite end of the gallery to the one by which they had entered were opened wide by two liveried servants. Nicholas slowly inhaled and put his shoulders back.

'Easy now,' Wilson whispered. 'Let me

speak, boy. You have nothing to be ashamed of.'

Nicholas watched as the two women entered the room: Amelia in a simple white day dress edged with the most delicate spring flowers the colour of sunshine, which suited her well; and her mother, who wore a heavier silk emerald-green classic style of gown. The colour, Nicholas thought, was very apt: it matched her jealous nature. One look from Elizabeth Pendleton and his heart skipped a beat. She still had a hold upon his heart, even though she had failed to break it when he was still a boy; but that same heart beat in a warmer and quicker way to the vision of Amelia, who positively glowed with joy at seeing him.

'Papa! Nicholas!' She almost skipped her steps toward them both. 'I've missed you both so much!' She stopped short as her mother's voice echoed down the gallery.

'Decorum, please, Amelia!'

The girl stopped, but Wilson stepped forward, held her outreached hands in greeting and gently kissed his precious daughter's cheek. 'Thank you, my dear.

You saved your papa's life,' he whispered so only she could hear. She smiled, but her eyes fixed upon Nicholas.

'You look well, Melly,' Nicholas said.

'Amelia!' Elizabeth snapped. 'Her name is Miss Amelia, but to you she has none.'

'Ma! Stop this please! People have been murdered and we are here, together — a family, as we should be.' Amelia smiled at them both.

Nicholas's eyes stared straight into Elizabeth's. She held his gaze, but the expression of disgust did not leave her face.

Wilson stepped in front of his wife. Nicholas had seen a movement in the gallery above and was far from easy that this meeting should take place with a witness looking on — especially if that witness was a magistrate.

'My dear, the shock of this horrid affair has been hard for you to take in. I can tell you are greatly distressed. You must stay calm, my dear, for we are here now and will see to your needs, as any good father and husband should.' He lowered his voice slightly, adding, 'And I am still your husband. So remember, sweet lady, that you still answer to me.' He coughed and raised his voice slightly so that all could hear as he continued. 'We come merely to reassure you that the murderer will soon be caught and that you and Amelia will be escorted to Mayfair to resume residence there in readiness for the Season, when our daughter will 'come out'. You will of course oversee this, with good grace, as any good mother should, won't you, my dear?' He tilted his head slightly to one side.

She seemed to take the masked warning from his words, as her manner, at least facially, changed. The eyes remained cold and detached, but she was no fool, and softened the hard line of her mouth into a pleasant line of acceptance.

'Of course I want only the best for our child, sir.' Her eyes glanced over Wilson's shoulder to Nicholas. She leaned closer to Wilson and whispered words that were only loud enough to drift across Wilson's shoulder to Nicholas's hearing: 'For 'we' have only one 'legitimate' child to consider.' She then stepped back.

Wilson turned and smiled at Amelia, who had not caught the last comment. 'Then we are agreed. We will join the escort in two days' time. You must excuse us now, for we have much to do, my dear Elizabeth, Amelia,' he said softly and stepped back.

Amelia stood before Nicholas. 'It is so good to see you . . . brother.' She gave him a quick hug before withdrawing, avoiding eye contact with her mother as she made her way down the gallery.

Elizabeth stepped forward; her mass of chestnut curls piled upon her head gave her a Romanesque profile. The Empress, Nicholas mused — for she would dearly have loved to have been one.

She must have taken the hint from Wilson, as she was keeping her manner pleasant for the benefit of any onlooker, but her eyes and words were direct. 'You dare to return at such a time as this?' Her voice was low, her manner and gestures light. She provided a vision of greeting, yet the words dripped with years of resentment. 'He called and you ran to his shirt-tails . . . Is that it?'

'I have, and I did. For what better time to be reunited than when my father needed my help and my family is under threat?' He held her gaze.

She laughed as if he had made a quip. Wilson had stopped not two paces away, listening and watching in a manner which appeared casual, but Nicholas knew was one that was desperate to catch every word.

'Isn't he big enough to look after himself, Nicholas? I heard you went by the name of 'Penn' when not in uniform. Can't quite justify the full name, Nicholas? Or are you ashamed of it?'

'Come, Nick, we must be on our way . . . Say goodbye to 'Mama' . . . ' Wilson said loudly, smiling at his wife, who remained impassive, but his eyes had taken on their old menace.

'I know who I am, lady, and I will protect my sister from harm as I would my father,' he whispered back, then bowed slightly. 'I wish you well, ma'am,' he said in an audible and polite manner.

She dipped her head slightly; a polite gesture, but it brought her closer to him momentarily. 'And I, sir, wish you dead, like all his bastards.' She smiled, turned and walked away, leaving Nicholas standing stock-still. She had had the final word and managed to shock him rigid. He knew that she resented Wilson bringing him into the house as a child and then acknowledging him as his son and heir, but he had no idea how deep her hatred of him went.

'Captain!' Wilson snapped him from his bemused thoughts. 'We have to go. Leave sentiment here, Nick, we have our duty to perform.'

'Yes, sir.' He followed Wilson as they bid the major good day, thanked him for the shelter and service he was providing, and arranged to see them two days hence, when they would be part of the escort to move the women back to the safety of the city.

* * *

Guy left the cottage and casually went to the edge of the woodland to pee. The woman, Gemma, had seen him do this, and seemed to accept that was all he was about. She continued bending and stacking wood. Wasting no time, he took to his heels at speed. He knew the direction that the madman and Mr Penn had gone off in. They had taken the roads to the grand hall. Molly had said roughly where it was when he asked what the place was like; he took to the fields, tracks and hedgerows, trying to avoid traps. He'd promised Mr Penn he would look after the man's back and he was going to.

★   ★   ★

Wilson and Nicholas rode away from the hall. Once out of sight from the building, Wilson led their horses into a clearing at the edge of the woods. It had a good vantage point over the vale. He dismounted, stood upon a cut tree stump and stared back at where they had just come from.

Nicholas tied his horse's reins next to Wilson's and stood on the grassy ground next to the stump. He looked up at the pained expression of the man he had always admired and loathed in equal measure throughout his life.

'It is time we talked, Nick. I want to know now, honestly, do you hate me as much as my wife does?' He stared down at Nicholas, who could not help but smile nervously.

'Could anyone hate you that much?'

'Not a good time for humour, boy. I asked a question and I need to know the answer to it.' For Wilson's face was tired and pale, more than it had been when Nicholas had found him in the lock-up cell.

'No, I cannot hate you . . . '

'Say it then . . . ' Wilson spoke softly, but genuinely.

'I do not hate you . . . Father, but I do not agree with much that you have done.' Nicholas flushed slightly; he had not used the term since being sent away to board at Elizabeth's insistence at such a young age, never to be allowed back to share his family home with his Melly, his half-sister whom he adored.

'I am sorry; I was away serving in India when the banker's draft I had sent back to your lovely mother was delayed. If you, your baby sister and she had not been sent to the debtor's prison, they would still have been with us now. The girl was weak and the mother delicate.' Wilson rubbed his tired eyes on the back of his sleeve. 'She was grievously wronged. I tried to put right a grave wrong by making you my heir and bringing you into my home, but Elizabeth was enraged when she found out that you existed. She could not conceive more children after Amelia and had failed to give me an heir. Once she discovered that you lived, she refused to go to my bed willingly. I tell you this as a man. Can you imagine what that rejection felt like? How was I to take it?

'I found Celia. I started again — tried to protect Amelia by not turning her mother out, and created what I hoped would be a loving family, as I had known briefly with your mother. Father insisted I married someone of my rank, you see, and I obeyed him on this, keeping my love safe, or so I thought. I was young, arrogant and foolish. I fell short of the task. Celia never loved me — I soon realised this — but she welcomed me to her bed, which my own wife did not. So you see how I created so much jealousy and disappointment. The only woman I was ever truly in love with and who loved me was your dear mother. I repeat my question, Nicholas.'

'My answer remains the same.'

'Your presence made Elizabeth's resentment grow, a daily reminder of my infidelity and her inability to have sons. She hated me for it. In my absence, her hatred focused upon your young shoulders. Worse, she could not accept that I had had a mistress who had provided a more joyous union than ours ever was.' He turned to face Nicholas. 'I realised that I could not leave you in her care.'

'I know. I remember the thrashings well.' Nicholas did. If he hated anyone, it was she, who had not even tried to understand his loss of a loving mother. So as a child he would vex her at every turn. If he was going to be thrashed for any imagined misdemeanour that came to her mind, he had childishly and foolishly decided he may as well give her a reason.

The battle of wills had begun — and also for Wilson's attention, when he was there.

'I was a soldier, Nick. I could not be at home. I sent you to get an education and bought you a commission to be with me as soon as I could.'

'So instead of thrashing the arrogance from me, you let the reality of war and a stiff training in survival stem the flow of anger. Yes, I realised this. I broke away from you last year, sir, in order to gain a perspective on it all. I do not resent you, but regret the past turned as it did. How many other 'bastards', as Elizabeth so eloquently describes us, do you have?' Nicholas watched his face half-smile in a resigned way.

'That I know of, just you. But you are my legal heir, Nicholas, so do not call yourself such. I have made it right with you.' He stepped down.

'There is no path I can take which will make it right between myself and Elizabeth, but you must allow Melly to have a happy life. Get her from under the woman's grip. She would not hurt her daughter, but she will cling and control her and eventually, I fear, embitter her also.'

'I intend to.'

'Tell me, Nick, what was her parting comment to you? Be honest, because I saw it cut you to the core.' Wilson asked his question, but his eyes glanced distractedly over Nicholas's shoulder. He flung them both to the floor as a bullet shot past, clipping the fabric of Nicholas's coat at the shoulder before splintering the bark of a tree opposite.

15

Both men sprang to their feet and made their way to the horses to retrieve their rifles before the gun could be reloaded and another shot could be set off. They threw their hats to the floor and headed into the cover of the forest, making their way toward the direction of where the shot came from.

Silently, they quickly made for a place of shelter. Loading their rifles with precision and speed, they set the sights and waited. There was one chance to get a shot off and it was Nicholas who managed to fire it. Then they ran like the devil was on their backs. Nicholas was sure he had struck his target, but when they heard a horse galloping off and could not get a clear view of the rider, they both swore.

Nicholas was the loudest. 'Did you see him? Was it Silas Mann? He told me that it was Granger who was dallying with your Nell. Let's get the horses and follow the bastard to town.'

Wilson was bending down. He was touching something.

'What is it?' Nicholas asked.

Wilson held out his thumb and forefinger. 'Blood. You did hit your man.'

'We got him!' Nicholas said.

'Perhaps,' Wilson remarked, a cold countenance sweeping over him.

Nicholas knew instantly he had missed something, some point that Wilson had not.

'Tell me?' Wilson prompted him.

'Silas said that your Nell and he . . . '

'What sweet words did she whisper into your ear, Nicholas?' Wilson's tone had regained an icy edge.

Nicholas knew he was referring back to Elizabeth. 'She wished me and your other bastards dead, Father.' He watched as a flicker of pain showed on Wilson's face.

'Never underestimate a woman, Nick.' Wilson pulled on his gloves and started back toward the horses.

'She is a woman. Her hate may be ripe but the murderer is definitely a man. You think she has been feeding information to Silas? You think she manipulates him or pays him? How could she? He owns the inn; she is hardly going to fraternise with his circles.' He caught up with Wilson. 'You brought us out here, laid a trap, and used us both as bait. You suspected her hand in this. Bloody hell, man! Can you not trust me to share what madness goes on in that damned brain of yours?' Nicholas was almost shouting.

They reached the horses and mounted. Wilson stared at Nicholas and turned his horse in a different direction, facing the way of the hall. 'Nicholas, you go to the town. Silas will have taken to his heels; follow the trail. I will get the major to send men; we will have him by nightfall.'

'And you?' Nicholas looked at the growing rage within Wilson's eyes.

'I will speak with my beloved.'

'What of Amelia?' Nicholas asked.

'She will be safe, and then you can return and act as her chaperone as you take her to Mayfair. I will join you both in a few days. It is time my wife and I were reconciled.'

Nicholas nodded. He did not want to stand in the middle of this last battle and he had no wish to know what Wilson planned; but it would be tempered, for Amelia still loved her mama, and Wilson would protect his daughter.

A movement in the woodland caught his eye. The rifle was raised and ready.

'Stop! Stop! It's me . . . Guy. I can help . . . I . . . ' Guy emerged panting, as he had been running for miles and was fit to drop. The shot had told him where he needed to be.

'You have no time for this,' Wilson said. 'Get Silas before the trail goes cold.'

'No . . . No . . . Wrong man!' He gasped for breath.

Both men looked at the boy, who was now standing by Nicholas's horse. 'It's the gamekeeper. His button were off his spare breeches. He makes 'em of bone — you know gamekeeper, he uses what he can. Not only that, but he goes away a few times of late, like when the women were murdered. Molly let it out. She does a lot of his mending and washing 'cos he kills the animals and gets in a right mess sometimes. He knew about your Nell, sir; they all did . . . Silas, he fancied her rotten, but she was not interested in him.'

Nicholas's face flushed. 'James had been adamant that the maid had seen something in the barn and entered out of curiosity, not that she knew the man who would take her life. But Sarah-Beth had no tie to you, did she?' He looked at Wilson.

Wilson shook his head. 'Elizabeth employed her.'

'She was always getting flirty with the men, James in particular, and upsetting Gemma,' Guy said. 'They rowed about it. Young Molly told me.'

Nicholas reached down and pulled the lad up onto the saddle. Both men rode toward the manor house.

They arrived under the cover of the forest tracks, and took cover in amongst the trees and watched the cottage. Time passed.

'Let the boy go back inside. They have no reason to suspect he has found us and he can let us know if James is there or not.' Wilson's voice was calm but cold, detached and devoid of any care for the boy's safety.

Nicholas realised the moment of fatherly affection had disappeared on the air, hidden behind the logistical mind of the colonel. Not to mention the vengeance, as yet unleashed, of a wronged man.

'No!' Nicholas answered straight away, but the lad ran out and made his way casually down toward the cottage.

Nicholas glared at Wilson.

'You sure he is not yours, Nicholas? He has the nerve of a Pendleton.'

'No, but he has little enough to live for. I think he is trying to prove his worth to us as a passage to a better life.' Nicholas watched, seeing that there was movement by the stables.

'Will you give him that better life?' Wilson asked without taking his eyes off the cottage.

Nicholas grinned fleetingly. 'Yes, I think I will.'

Both men made their way down, staying to the shadows and to the cover at the back of the stables. They heard a rider approach and enter the building. Nicholas stepped inside, ducking low.

Amelia was walking out of a stall, having left her horse by the fresh hay. In her finest riding attire, she was beautiful. Nicholas's sudden appearance made her jump.

'Whatever are you doing here, Nicholas?' she asked quickly.

He straightened up and Wilson followed him in, having heard his daughter's voice.

'What are you doing here, Amelia?' Nicholas asked in return, glancing around to make sure that no one else was there.

'I forgot some jewellery when we had to leave so suddenly with the major. Mama said I could collect it when I delivered her note to James and bid Gemma and the children goodbye.' She smiled at them both but, as she looked from one to the other, her smile faded. 'What is wrong, Nick?' she asked.

Wilson came forward. 'Give me the note. Elizabeth allowed you to do this deed unescorted?'

Without hesitating, she put her hand in

her pocket and pulled out the folded paper. 'Well, she said that I would be safe and the soldiers were on patrol anyway. She assured me I would not come to any harm.'

Wilson opened it and read it, before passing it to Nicholas. James's education was limited, so it had been plainly written.

Remove the last problem. Look in box under second planter in day room. Do not fail. He must be found guilty.

Nicholas passed it back to Wilson.

'Amelia, stay here,' Wilson told her. 'We will return shortly. You must not leave this building until one of us calls for you. Your mother is . . . unwell. She is in need of a long rest. Her mind troubles her with falsehoods. She will be visiting a spa whilst Nicholas takes you to London in a private carriage. There will be no need for a guard. All will be well again. I will join you there. Stay here — promise me?'

'Yes, Papa . . . Mother's 'illness', it will get better, won't it? I will see her again, won't I?' Amelia's pained expression showed Nicholas that she was indeed worried for her. She may not know the truth, but the young woman must have sensed something was sadly amiss. Nicholas realised how astute the girl was and how brave. She was choosing her words carefully. The writing was not Amelia's — of that he was relieved, for he knew it well. She was the true innocent in all of this business. She must have known there was something wrong with the woman's moods, but thankfully she would have no notion as to what it was.

'In time,' he said quietly. 'You wait here.'

★   ★   ★

Guy entered the cottage after knocking gently upon the door. The family was seated around the table. Molly's face was a bit flushed and her pa's face looked a little drained, which was nothing to the wan colour on Gemma's.

'Sorry I took so long. I like the country — not used to it, just wanted to run. Were the peas alright?' He smiled and Molly returned his goodwill, but the parents only exchanged concerned looks. 'Can I still wait with thee? Mr Penn is taking a long time.'

'Aye,' James said. 'Sit yourself down.'

He did so, on the small stool by the fire, and noticed a strip of cloth had been dropped by the mother's chair. It had a blood stain upon it. He had the answer, but realised he had not thought the situation through as to what he was to do next about warning Mr Penn and the madman.

* * *

Wilson found the money left in the box for James's 'troubles' . . . Blood money. He put it in his pocket with the note. 'It should pay for her . . . treatment.'

Nicholas raised an eyebrow.

'She is obviously mad. I will not have Amelia's name dragged through the courts because of the ravings of her mother. No, she will be treated privately in a suitable establishment where her delusions will be kept away from the world. If she behaves well she may get to see her grandchildren,

186

but I would not hold out much hope on that.'

'Now for James!' Nicholas said. 'What of the family, sir?'

'He should have thought of that. The woman has been covering for her man. The children will be looked after by the parish charity.'

'The poorhouse?' Nicholas said, knowing how bleak they could be.

'It is more than he offered Nell and the other wenches. Come, man! Think like a soldier. We are at war. He has killed, and would have killed you and framed me.'

Nicholas nodded. His old friend was his new enemy: betrayal of the lowliest kind. The wenches could not fight back. However, as soldiers they could.

★　★　★

The cottage door flew open. Nicholas and Wilson burst in, pistols drawn; but unseen below the table, James already had his loaded and on his knee ready. A gamekeeper has plenty of weapons.

Wilson glared at him. Molly screamed.

Nicholas looked at Guy. 'Take the children to the house and stay there.'

Gemma grabbed the baby. 'What is the meaning of this? Why are you here?'

'Tell her, James, if she really does not know,' Wilson ordered.

'Take the children to the house as he said, woman. I have business to discuss here.'

'But . . . '

'Do it!'

A look of resignation swept across her face. She gave the baby to Molly and looked at Guy. 'Take them. I'm staying here with my man. GO!'

Nicholas looked at Guy. 'Take them to the house . . . go on.' The lad nodded and as Molly sobbed, utterly bemused, helped to carry the other children between them to the manor.

Wilson stared at James. 'Why?'

There was blood starting to seep through James's shirt above his waist. Nicholas realised his shot had hit home. The man's face was pale. Gemma put her hand upon her man's shoulder.

'You were never here. She wanted to be

188

free of your curse, she said. You played freely with the daughter of Eve and that beautiful woman could know no other man. I found out about your wench — I told her. She was trapped; we were all trapped.' His blank eyes stared back.

'You'd rape and kill, just because Elizabeth was lonely?' Nicholas said incredulously.

'She threatened to turn us out! No money, and no references and . . . she knew about . . . '

'What?' Wilson snapped.

Gemma looked boldly at Wilson. 'He'd been wrongly accused of messing with a girl a few years back, when he took some pheasants to market. In a place far away from here. The girl had lied.'

Nicholas saw the fleeting grimace of guilt cross her husband's face, unobserved by Gemma. She continued. 'He never touched her, and then she died — fell off an icy bridge. He was hounded. Mrs Pendleton sent a letter of good character and gave a donation to the girl's family. All was put right, but we owed her.'

James stared at Nicholas. 'She showed

me how it was wrong — lust and
. . . begetting bastards. If only you had
not come to him, Mr Nicholas . . . '

Wilson glared sheer hatred. 'I would
have hung for the girls' murders as my
alias. The Pendleton name would have
held. No doubt Nicholas's turn would
have been another unfortunate accident
in the not-so-distant future. You simple-
ton — did you not realise she would have
set you up with no trail back to her?'
Wilson stepped forward, pointing the
pistol. 'Stand, fool! My identity would
have come out, but you would have been
suspected once your past was revealed.
My dear wife would only need to whisper
into the major's ear in her distress and
you, too, would have hung, after my death
of course, and once the horror of my
double life had been discovered.'

'Let her go.' James nodded to Gemma,
who gripped his shoulder.

'She covered for you . . . ' Wilson said.

'You really are a bastard. We have four
children. She was right,' James said.

'I had three!' Wilson snapped back.

James shifted his position on the chair,

grimacing with pain. He glanced up at his Gemma, who tearfully smiled back down at him and closed her eyes as the flash of his pistol took her life. Nicholas tried to grab the other gun from the man's hands but he fired it at point-blank range into his own chest. Two bodies lay atop one another on the cottage's earthen floor, united in death as they were in life; dead to sin, they would answer to a higher authority now.

Nicholas placed his hand upon Wilson's shoulder. 'Come, it's over. No more girls will die at the sadist's hands. Amelia needs us both. We'll send the militia in to clear up the mess.'

Once outside in the cool night air, they stared at each other. Amelia ran out of the house; having heard the children's cries, she had gone to help.

'Are they both dead? Did you . . . ?' She looked anxiously from father to son.

'No, James did,' Nicholas said quietly.

'Was it really James?' She hugged her father.

'Yes,' he said simply, patting her back.

'Then you must see the children are

well looked after. It is not their fault, Father,' she pleaded. 'You cannot hold the father's deeds against them.'

He looked at Nicholas over her head, who responded with a raised eyebrow.

'Promise, Papa?'

'Very well, I promise. They will be given a new home with people who will care properly for them. My word upon it. They will have a chance to be good people — their choice. But you must trust me on this and look to your own future. Let loose all ties with this place, Amelia. Your future is elsewhere with us, or your husband, whoever he may be.'

'Yes, very well. Do what you must do, Father. I will keep the children in the house with me and young Guy, until all is settled. Be quick though, please, because they are indeed shocked and distressed. You must get them away from here.' She kissed her father's cheek and ran back into her old home.

'Nicholas, stay with her. Leave the major and Elizabeth to me.'

'Yes,' Nicholas said, and he watched a tired-looking man mount his horse.

'Say it again, Nicholas Pendleton.'

Nicholas grinned. 'Yes, Father, I will.'

'Good man, my son!' he answered proudly. But as he focused on the road ahead, the glint of cold madness crept back into his eyes, and Nicholas tried hard not to feel even the slightest pang of remorse for the justice Wilson was about to mete out to Elizabeth, his estranged wife.

We do hope that you have enjoyed reading this large print book.

Did you know that all of our titles are available for purchase?

We publish a wide range of high quality large print books including:
Romances, Mysteries, Classics
General Fiction
Non Fiction and Westerns

Special interest titles available in large print are:
The Little Oxford Dictionary
Music Book, Song Book
Hymn Book, Service Book

Also available from us courtesy of Oxford University Press:
Young Readers' Dictionary
(large print edition)
Young Readers' Thesaurus
(large print edition)

For further information or a free brochure, please contact us at:
Ulverscroft Large Print Books Ltd.,
The Green, Bradgate Road, Anstey,
Leicester, LE7 7FU, England.
Tel: (00 44) **0116 236 4325**
Fax: (00 44) **0116 234 0205**